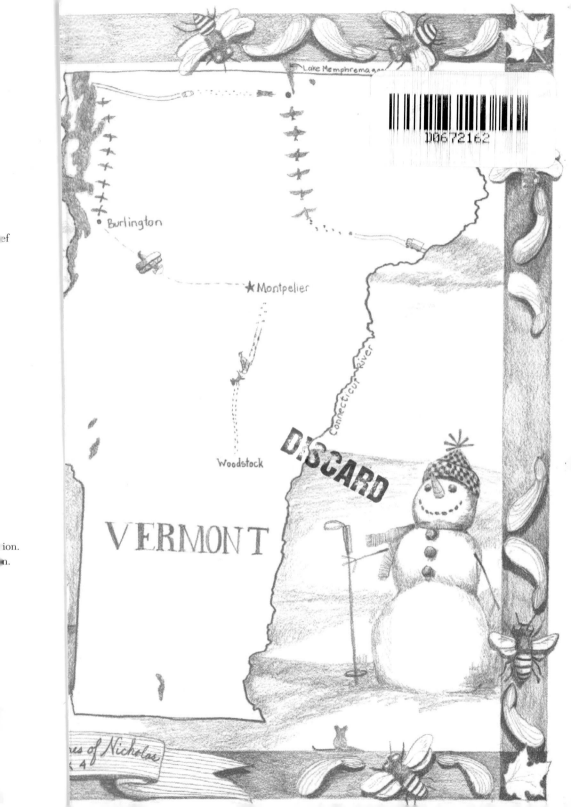

All inquiries should be addressed to:
Mitten Press
An imprint of Ann Arbor Media Group LLC
2500 S. State Street
Ann Arbor, MI 48104

Printed and bound at Edwards Brothers, Inc., Ann Arbor, Michigan

10   9   8   7   6   5   4   3   2   1

Library of Congress Cataloging-in-Publication Data

Arenstam, Peter.
Nicholas : a Vermont tale / by Peter Arenstam ;
illustrated by Karen Busch Holman.
p. cm.
Summary: Having found the family journal he was seeking,
Nicholas continues on to Vermont in hopes of reuniting with his paren
ISBN 978-1-58726-522-8 (hardcover : alk. paper) [1. Voyages and travels--[
2. Adventure and adventurers--Fiction. 3. Mice--Fiction. 4. Animals--Fic
5. Vermont--Fiction.] I. Busch Holman, Karen, 1960- ill. II. Title.
PZ7.A6833Nr 2010 [Fic]--dc22
2009049628

Book design by Danny Nanos

Chapter One

Nicholas, Edward, and Francis floated on the Upper Ammonoosuc River in an old Tupperware container they had found along the shore. They looked at each other in the bright sunlight. Nicholas had been searching for his cousin Francis for a long time. With his friend Edward, Nicholas had come all the way from western Massachusetts, through Maine and New Hampshire to find the family journal that Francis carried.

Francis kept his paw on the battered book as they drifted on the current. The three animals were on their way to Vermont. They were looking for another member of their mouse family to help them with the journal.

"I can't believe we have found you at last," Nicholas said. He smiled and shook his fuzzy brown head.

"What have I been telling you, Nicholas?" Edward said. "I just knew we would catch up with your cousin. It may have taken a bit longer than I predicted, but we did it." Edward the chipmunk tried to stand up to make his point. Their makeshift boat rocked deeply from side to side.

"Sit down, Edward. We don't want to end up in the river," Nicholas said to his boastful friend.

"Remember," Francis said, "it is our family journal. I have as much right to it as you do, Nicholas."

"Of course you do, Francis," Nicholas said. "All I want to do is bring home a copy of the journal to my family."

Nicholas lived with his mother and father on a farm in western Massachusetts. For many years, the family recorded events important to them in a journal, but their mouse family journal had been ruined in a flood. Nicholas had set out in search of a copy of the journal.

The three small animals sat quietly in the plastic box drifting with the current down the river. They passed stands of trees and green fields on the shore. The river wandered its way around wide bends and passed pinched-off oxbows. In the distance, there was a steady roaring sound.

Edward sat with his eyes closed. He never did like boat travel. Francis kept looking from Nicholas to

Edward. Their boat was now rushing along and water splashed over the sides. Francis held the journal high to keep it dry. Nicholas stood up and looked ahead to see where they were going.

"Edward, this doesn't look right," Nicholas said.

Edward tried to stand up. He felt dizzy and tired. "I can't look, Nicholas, what is happening?"

"There is something blocking the river up ahead. The water is moving faster, the river is getting narrower, and there is lots of spray in the air," Nicholas said.

Francis popped up over the edge of their boat. "What is that noise, Nicholas?" It was getting louder. "Will the journal be safe?"

Nicholas looked ahead and realized what was coming. There was no time to lose. They had to do something fast. "Edward, you have to help. There is a dam ahead. If we don't get off the river, we are going to be swept over the dam."

Edward got to his feet. He might not like boat travel but he liked even less the idea of going over the dam. He reached over the side and started paddling as fast as he could. Nicholas paddled on the other side.

Francis held tightly to the journal. "Hurry," he said, "we are getting closer."

"You have got to help us, Francis," Nicholas said. "The river current is pulling us toward the dam."

"I have to keep the journal safe, Nicholas. It is the only copy left."

"We won't be around to read it if you don't help us, Francis," Nicholas said.

"Nicholas is right," Edward said. "You must help us now. There is a chance we can make it to that old tree." Edward continued to paddle furiously. There was a dead tree leaning out over the water in front of the dam. The top-most branches just touched the water.

"Yes, Edward," Nicholas said, "we have to steer toward the tree. We can grab the branches before we get swept over the dam. We need your help to steer, Francis."

Francis, who still clutched the journal to his chest, could see there was no other way. He carefully moved toward the back of the boat and put the journal at his feet. It took him a few attempts to figure out how to steer. He used his paws to paddle first one way, then another, to keep the boat on course.

"I think we are going to make it," Nicholas shouted. They were getting closer and closer to the tree.

"Don't stop now," Edward said. "We have to keep paddling."

The roar of the water over the dam was loud. They could see the rushing stream spilling over the top. White foam and spray leapt in the air all along the leading edge of the cement dam.

The three animals paddled and steered the boat so that it would pass just under the branches of the tree. Nicholas looked up. When the first branch passed by overhead, he leaped and stretched out his arms. His paws gripped the loose bark and held on tightly. He was safe.

Next it was Edward's turn. He reached up as the next branch swept past. Edward gripped the branch. The bark of the dead tree slipped loose of the branch as Edward held onto it. He started to fall back into the boat. Nicholas was there to grab him. He tugged with all his might and pulled Edward up onto the tree.

"Francis," Nicholas shouted over the rushing water, "pass up the journal, then we will pull you up." Francis held the journal in his paws. He didn't want to let go of it.

"No, you two can pull me up with the journal."

"You're too heavy. We will take the journal, then you can get out of the boat."

Nicholas reached down and had his paws on the canvas-wrapped book. Francis pulled it away from Nicholas.

"I will protect it," Francis said. "Hurry, we don't have much time. Pull me up!"

Nicholas and Edward had no choice. They both tugged on Francis and the journal. It was too much. The boat started to shift in the water. The river current was pulling it toward the dam.

Francis looked at Nicholas and Edward. He sat down in the boat, the journal protected by his front legs.

The boat spun free of the tree and out into the river current. Francis kept his eyes on the journal. Nicholas and Edward watched from the shore.

"Francis, watch out," Nicholas shouted. The boat tipped over the edge of the dam and was lost from sight in the foam and spray.

Chapter Two

Nicholas and Edward bounded off the tree. They ran along the bank, calling for Francis. The roar of the water and the splashing made it hard to hear.

At the edge of the dam, Nicholas could see down to the river below. It was not a very tall dam. What seemed liked an endless fall from the upper river was really just a short drop to the level below.

Edward came puffing up from behind. "I must say, Nicholas, there is never a dull moment when traveling with you, my friend. Can you see Francis?"

The two animals looked down the river. They could just make out a white speck bobbing in the current, heading for the mouth of the small river.

"That must be him," Nicholas said. "He made it over the dam." Nicholas pointed at the Tupperware box twirling along in the rapids. "He is still clutching the journal," Nicholas added.

"Well, he is headed on to Vermont without us," Edward said. "We will never catch him on land."

The two small animals stood on the bank of the river, wondering what to do now. A sleek river otter appeared next to them.

"Your friend took quite a ride. Wasn't he brave, riding over the dam like that? I've lived on rivers all my life and there's one thing my old ma taught us—be careful of dams."

Nicholas and Edward jumped back from the unexpected animal. They hadn't heard him approach.

"You're lucky the water level is high. Later in the summer, the bottom of the dam will be all rocks and logs and whatnot. Not a soft landing, I can assure you," the otter said. He clicked his tongue and shook his head.

"Francis never meant to go over the dam," Nicholas said. "We are trying to get to Vermont. The dam kind of surprised us, that's all."

"You're headed to Vermont, you say?" the otter asked. "I live in Vermont, myself. Born and raised right outside of St. Johnsbury, you know. That's the gateway to the northeast kingdom. It's the prettiest part of the state, if I do say so myself. You better jump right in and catch up with your friend."

"We can't do that," Nicholas said. "We can't swim that fast."

"Or for that long," Edward said. "Besides, the water is a bit chilly for swimming, don't you think?"

"I swim in the river no matter the season. That is, if the ice hasn't covered up the water," the otter said.

"What about Francis? Where does this river go?" Nicholas asked. He had traveled a long way looking for his cousin and he didn't want to lose him again.

"Well, he's headed for the Connecticut River downstream a bit," the otter said. "That river makes the whole eastern border between Vermont and New Hampshire. There's no telling where in Vermont he will go when he reaches the Connecticut River."

"We can't lose him again," Nicholas said.

"Now leave it to me, Nicholas," Edward started. "I've gotten you out of more trouble than I can remember. Let me just think a moment."

"You better not take too much time there, Mr. Chipmunk," the otter said. "I don't see your friend on the river any longer. He could be in Vermont already."

"Edward, we have to get going," Nicholas said. "We have to catch up with Francis. We can't swim fast enough to catch up with him."

"Besides," Edward added, "we have no idea where he might be going. Francis is looking for some answers to questions he read about in the journal."

"Now, I don't know where he would go, but I do know that there is a museum in St. Johnsbury, right near the border. Your cousin could discover many things about Vermont there. I tell you what, let me call on a friend and we'll give you a ride. You'll catch up with your cousin in no time."

"Now, now, we don't want you to go to any trouble. I don't even see any of your friends around here," Edward said. He backed away from the water. For all his traveling, Edward really didn't like to be uncomfortable.

"No trouble, I am sure," the otter said. "Why, I have friends anywhere there is a bit of running water. I won't be half a minute." The otter raced away much faster than either Nicholas or Edward expected. The two animals stood looking at each other.

"Hello again! I told you I wouldn't be a minute. This is Edgar. He lives in New Hampshire. I'm Oscar, by the way. Now let's go."

Without saying another word, the two sleek otters ducked under the small animals, perched them on their backs, and dove into the river. Even with the extra weight, the otters were excellent swimmers.

Nicholas and Edward had all they could do to hold on as the otters slid through the water. The spray from the two otters flew all around them. When they did manage to look up, they saw they were headed over the same dam Francis went over earlier.

Chapter Three

Without hesitating, the otters plunged over the dam. The rushing water carried them out and over the cement. Nicholas and Edward clung to the backs of the sleek animals. They dove into the deep pool of water at the base of the dam. Nicholas kept his eyes open and his mouth shut, but Edward forgot to do both.

When they broke the surface, Nicholas shouted with glee. Edward coughed, and wheezed, and blinked. The two otters just laughed and kept swimming.

In time they reached the mouth of the river and

climbed out of the upper Ammonoosuc. The broad Connecticut River flowed past them. A busy road through the hilly farmland followed the river down the New Hampshire side.

"Now, there you go," Oscar said. "You follow this road into Lancaster where it turns toward Vermont. That will take you right into St. Johnsbury."

Nicholas smoothed down his whiskers and brushed water off his fur.

Edward hopped on one paw trying to force water out of his ear. "I can't hear a thing," he said. "Remind me never to do that again, Nicholas."

The otters smiled and jumped back in the river. "You take care now. Look for a ride headed into St. Johnsbury. Trucks for Maple Grove Farms will be coming by now and again."

In time they saw a big, old box truck lumbering along the road. It bounced and rumbled as it wound its way around sharp corners and over the lumpy farm country. A herd of black and white cows wandered along a fence in a nearby field.

Nicholas and Edward ran up to the slow-moving animals. "Hello, ladies," Nicholas said, "I was wondering if you could help us out?"

The lead cow chewed a bit, then looked down at the small mouse. "What can we do for you, little one?" she asked.

Nicholas explained what he wanted and gave the cows his best sad-mouse look.

"Ah, how could we say no to such a cute little thing?" the cow said. "Follow me ladies," she said to the rest of the herd.

The cows turned from their path along the fence, stepped over a low hanging piece of fencing, and wandered down into the road. One after another, the cows collected in a bunch. They filled the road from side-to-side. Nicholas and Edward watched from the tall grass.

The truck slowed to a stop in front of the cows. The driver leaned out the window and waved his cap at the cows. The cows stared back, slowly chewed on some grass, and then surrounded the vehicle. The driver beeped his horn.

Nicholas and Edward ran to the back of the truck and the lead cow gave Nicholas and Edward a boost up onto the back of the truck.

"There you go, little fellas," the cow said. "Now we better get moving before the driver gets really mad."

"Thank you," Nicholas said. "You were kind to help us."

The cows slowly moved on, heading for the barn. The truck driver gave one long, last annoyed beep and he drove away. Nicholas and Edward held on, hoping to get to St. Johnsbury in time to catch up with Francis.

The scent of something sweet and delicious drifted out to the hungry pair. "Nicholas," Edward said, "I am so hungry. I do hope we find your cousin quickly. I have the strangest craving for pancakes."

Nicholas listened to his belly rumble, but he said nothing.

The truck slowed down as it came to a town with brick buildings lining both sides of the street. Busy people were going and coming. The truck stopped for a moment to let a family cross the street and Nicholas and Edward hopped off. The family headed to a big brick building with a tall tower in front.

Edward could smell the lunch wrapped up in a bag carried by one of the children. "Hmm," he sniffed. "Let's follow them. I am so hungry that I could eat everything in that lunch bag."

The two animals skipped along the curb trying to stay out of sight. They managed to follow the family into the building before the big door clanged shut.

Inside, glass-lined cases were set up around the big open room. The children ran from case to case, shouting their discoveries to each other.

Edward couldn't keep up with the child with the lunch, and so he wandered through the building on his own. He came to a case labeled "Vermont Wetlands." Inside, animals seemed to be standing still in different poses. Edward thought these animals might be able to help him find Nicholas's cousin. They might even have some food they would share with him.

Edward found a way to scramble up the back. He peered over the side of the dark case. He waved to a raccoon perched next to a stream. "Hello there," Edward waved his paw.

The raccoon didn't respond.

Edward leaned out and waved again. "I said 'Hello.' I don't mean to interrupt but my friend and I are quite hungry."

Edward leaned over farther. He waved his paws at the still raccoon. She seemed to be ignoring him, Edward thought. He hopped up and down, chittering away. Waving his paws, he lost his balance. He spun his front legs around, trying to keep from falling.

It was too late. Edward tumbled inside the glass case. He rolled to a stop next to the raccoon. She didn't move when he bumped into her.

Edward looked up. He was inside the big glass case with no way out. He didn't see which way Nicholas had gone, and none of the animals in the case could help him.

Chapter Four

Nicholas and Edward had wandered into the Fairbanks Museum in St. Johnsbury, Vermont.

Nicholas was at one end of the great hall staring at a polar bear. He had never seen a white bear like this

before. Bears he knew were only this still when they hibernated. Then, he heard his friend Edward's voice.

"Edward?" Nicholas squeaked. "What's happened, Edward?" Nicholas scurried along the edge of the room trying to locate his friend. He could hear a tap, tap, tapping coming from one end of the room. Looking up, he saw a long glass case taking up one end of the room.

Edward's face was pressed against the glass. Nicholas could not make out Edward's muffled words. A fox, ducks, and even a beaver stood posed around Edward.

"What are you doing in there?" Nicholas asked his friend.

Edward started to explain but Nicholas could not understand what he said. Nicholas shook his head. Edward tapped on the glass. He jumped up as if to reach the top of the case. He tried to keep an eye on the animals surrounding him.

"Don't worry, Edward, I will find a way to get you out. I don't think you have to worry about those animals."

Edward couldn't climb up the slick sides of the glass case, and Nicholas couldn't climb in from the outside. There was no one nearby to help.

If Nicholas were to get his friend out, he would have to find a way to do it himself. He scurried away, twitching his nose, thinking and looking as he ran. Edward sat down inside the case wondering where his friend was going. The animals around him continued to stare in one direction without speaking.

Suddenly the lights went out and the big main door clanged shut. They were closing the museum.

Nicholas found a spiral staircase tucked into one side of the big room. He circled around and around, climbing to the second floor, which looked out over the main floor. He thought maybe he could see down into the case and find a way to help his friend.

From the railing, Nicholas peered down at Edward. He felt sad and alone. He just couldn't find a way to help his friend. The quiet, empty museum echoed Nicholas's long sigh.

While he sat with his head in his paws, he heard a noise from the main floor. He peered over the edge of the railing again and saw a small animal nosing about.

Nicholas jumped from his seat, slid down the spiral staircase railing, and landed with a bump on the shiny wood floor.

"Who's there?" the animal asked. "The museum is closed now, you shouldn't be here." An old mouse turned to go about his business.

"Don't go," Nicholas said. "I need your help. My friend is trapped in one of these glass cases. I can't get him out."

"What's that, you say? Your friend wants to get in one of my cases? Why, that's not allowed. Like I said, the museum's closed."

"No, no," Nicholas said. "He doesn't want to get into one of the cases. He wants to get OUT. He's trapped inside." Nicholas tugged on the old mouse's paw. "Please come with me. I'll show you."

"Never heard of such a thing. We don't allow live animals in our cases," the old mouse said. "I've been watching things in this museum at night for years. Never heard of any of these animals wanting to get out."

"You don't understand," Nicholas said. "My friend Edward is a live chipmunk. He fell into the case. He is too small to climb out over the top."

"Now, why didn't you say so?" the old mouse asked. "We can get him out of the door in the back. Each case has a door so the museum workers can clean them."

"That's great," Nicholas said. "Will you open the door and let my friend out?"

"No, I can't do that," the old mouse shrugged.

"Why not?" Nicholas asked.

"All the doors on the cases are locked, you know. You need the keys to open the door."

"You never said the doors were locked," Nicholas said. "Why didn't you tell me?"

"Well, you never asked," the old mouse said. "I tell you what, you help me check on the rest of the museum and I'll show you where the keys are. It's going to take some figuring on how we are going to use them." The old mouse shook his grey whiskers and scurried on his way.

Nicholas sighed and followed along. He hoped Edward wouldn't worry too much waiting for him.

Chapter Five

Morgan was an old mouse but he moved quickly among the exhibits. "Upstairs there are all sorts of things from all around the world," Morgan said. "We don't have time to look up there now. I'll show you where the keys to the cases are kept. You will have to figure out how to use them."

Morgan scurried right up to the front desk where they sold tickets during the day. He climbed up the edge of the desk, followed by Nicholas, and perched on the top.

"Now, here's the problem," Morgan said. "The keys you need are locked in the cabinet." The front of the desk had a locked wooden door, behind which were kept all sorts of keys used in the museum.

If he had plenty of time, Nicholas thought, a mouse could gnaw a perfectly useful hole in the bottom of the door. He was sure Edward didn't want to wait that long. He rummaged around on the desk.

"Aha," he said. "I bet I can do something with this." He held a big silver paper clip. "If you help me bend it, I can get the door open."

"I'm not so sure," Morgan said, but he held one end of the clip while Nicholas pulled and pried one end out.

"There," Nicholas said, "all we have to do is push this in and twist it around. The door is bound to pop open."

"It will never work," Morgan said. He wandered off on the rest of his rounds.

Nicholas took the paper clip and pushed it into the lock. He tried twisting and turning it. The clip bent a little but nothing else happened. It was getting late. He stood on the part of the clip that stuck out and started to bounce up and down. The door creaked a little. The clip was springy. Nicholas bounced more.

"I think it is going to open," Nicholas said. As he moved, the lock made a click, then another, and the door sprung open. Nicholas flew through the air. "Look out below," he shouted as he sailed out over the edge of the desk. He landed in a heap on top of Morgan.

"Well, you certainly make yourself at home, don't you?" Morgan said. The two mice were in a ball.

"I am so sorry, Morgan," Nicholas said, "but I got the door open. Can we get the keys now?"

Morgan was a bit rumpled and none too pleased with this mouse from out-of-state, but he fished out the key Nicholas needed. They scampered back to Edward, who tapped on the glass again.

"Now, where is the lock to the case?" Nicholas asked Morgan.

From the floor of the museum, Morgan pointed up. Far over their heads, Nicholas could see the lock. He sat down in despair. There was no way he could get the heavy set of keys up to the lock. Once more he felt he was at a dead end.

Morgan stood next to him. "I tried to tell you," Morgan said. "That lock is just about as far out of reach as the stars in the sky."

Nicholas perked up. He couldn't give up on his friend. They had been in many tight spots before and always managed to find a way out. He had to find a way to get the keys up to the lock.

Nicholas noticed a string of balloons left over from a birthday party earlier that day. The balloons were tied to a chair leg so they wouldn't float up to the barrel-vaulted ceiling. "Morgan, I think I have figured out how to get the keys up to the lock."

Nicholas dragged the ring of keys over to where the balloons were tied. He made sure Morgan showed him which key would open the lock. He held that in his paws. "Now Morgan, can you untie the balloons one by one and tie them to these keys?"

"Why, of course I can. I learned knots back when I was just a young mouse. Used to tie the house cat's whiskers in a knot when he was sleeping," Morgan chuckled.

Nicholas stood looking up at the case as Morgan switched the balloons from the chair to the key ring. After a few balloons, the keys began to bounce on the floor. With a few more balloons, Nicholas had to hold the keys or they would float up to the ceiling.

Finally, with all the balloons tied onto the ring, Nicholas lifted up into the air. "Ha, ha," Nicholas shouted. He twitched his tail this way and that.

"Well, I'll be jigged," Morgan said. "I have never seen a flying mouse before. Steer over to the lock now." Morgan could see Nicholas was using his tail like a rudder on a plane. Nicholas rose up and up. He needed to get the key into the lock or he would keep on rising up to the ceiling with no way down.

He switched his tail a little to the right. He drifted to the left. He switched his tail a little to the left. He drifted to the right. The lock was just ahead. His whiskers quivered. The lock was right in front of him. He pushed the key into the lock.

"I did it!" he shouted. He stood on the key and it spun around. The door popped open. "Hello, Edward," Nicholas said to his newly freed friend.

"Nicholas, if anyone can rescue an animal from a cage, it is you, my friend," Edward said.

Chapter Six

Edward jumped out of the glass case and hugged his friend. With his weight added to that of Nicholas, who was still holding onto the balloons, they both floated to the floor. Nicholas let go of the balloons, which immediately rose up to the wood-covered arched ceiling.

"There are going to be some questions around here in the morning," Morgan said. "It might be best if you two take off now."

"I, for one, am more than ready to leave," Edward said. "However, where exactly are we going to go? Francis wasn't here and we don't have any clues as to where he might be."

"Well, I tell you what, if your cousin is looking for someone who knows a few things about Vermont, he might head north. If it is history he is interested in, the state capital is the place, or even all the way to Lake Champlain. Lots of state history surrounding that lake. Yes, sir."

Morgan led Nicholas and Edward to the basement where exhibits about stars and weather waited for the day's visitors. "I have my own entrance to the museum down here," Morgan said. A wood-framed cellar window had a neat round hole chewed through it. "Right this way, boys, and thanks for visiting my museum," Morgan said. "It will be light soon and I suspect you'll want to rest up today before your trip west."

The darkness outside was giving way to the sun rising beyond the hills of town. Birds called out to each other and a truck rumbled along the road into town. Nicholas and Edward thanked their new friend and looked for a safe place to sleep and find some food before they continued their travels.

When they woke from their rest and dined on some tasty maple seeds, they discussed their plans. "I have been away from my family too long," Nicholas said. "My parents must be so worried. What if Uncle William didn't make it out to their farm to tell my parents where I am?"

Nicholas had spent some time with his uncle on Martha's Vineyard. When Nicholas went off to Maine to search for his cousin Francis, William had said he would go to western Massachusetts to tell Nicholas's parents where he had gone.

"Now Nicholas, think how happy your parents will be when you return with the lost family journal," Edward said. "You will have all your old family stories back and everyone will be reunited."

"I just don't know how we are ever going to find my cousin in this hilly state," Nicholas said.

"I can't believe I am going to suggest this, but we should try and catch a ride with a bird that knows the area well. You know how I feel about flying," Edward said. He had really dreaded the times they had gotten rides from birds. Edward always put up a brave front, but he never seemed to find joy in flying the way Nicholas did.

The sun had made its way across the sky and was sinking below the hills to the west. The two animals felt the need to keep moving. They made their way out of town and quickly found themselves on a country road following a valley between two ranges of hills. It was nearing dark, the time that many birds and animals like to be out and about. Nicholas and Edward walked near an old stone wall. A row of ancient maple trees interrupted the line of the wall now and again.

Edward was about to say something about stopping for the night when a large, fluttery bird landed right across the wall from them. Nicholas and Edward jumped.

"There's a delicious batch of seeds on this side of the wall," the wild turkey called out as she twisted her long neck to see over the wall. "Oh, pardon me," the turkey said. "I didn't see you two there when I landed. I must say," she went on, "you two look tasty." The turkey bent over and examined the mouse and the chipmunk closely.

Edward and Nicholas backed up and looked for cover in the stone wall. "We are most decidedly not tasty," Edward said. "Besides, I didn't think turkeys ate animals like us."

The turkey straightened up and blinked its narrow little eyes once or twice. "Ah, you're right, you're right.

I'm always forgetting things like that." The turkey next looked down at its claws. There were maple seeds sticking between the talons. "I do remember I like maple seeds." She pecked at the seeds.

"Gertie," the turkey called over the wall, "you must try the seeds over here." A second turkey fluttered over the wall landing between Nicholas and Edward.

"These aren't maple seeds, Sadie," Gertie said. "You caught yourself a mouse and chipmunk. We don't eat those, remember?"

Sadie sighed and lifted one talon to show her friend the maple seeds. "I remember that. I'm talking about these seeds." The two turkeys pecked away at the ground for a few minutes, chewing and swallowing the abundant seeds.

Nicholas and Edward scooted out of the path of the hungry birds. They looked at each other, wondering if they could dare ask these two for a ride. There seemed to be no other form of transportation available. Nicholas decided he better speak up and explain what he needed.

Chapter Seven

icholas approached the first turkey. "Hello, there," he said. "My friend and I need some help."

The two turkeys, busy eating, had forgotten the small animals were nearby.

"Oh, my," Sadie said. "Who are you? You startled me. Gertie, would you look at this little mouse? Isn't he cute?"

"Cute?" Gertie said. "You wanted to eat him just a few minutes ago."

"I would never want to eat such a cute little mouse. And who is your friend hiding over there?" Sadie asked.

"That's Edward. We need some help." Nicholas tried to explain to the confused birds what they needed.

"Now, let me see," Sadie said, as she scratched at the ground. "You want us to look for your cousin. What was his name again?"

"No, no," Nicholas said "we don't want you to look for Francis. We need you to take us north from here. You know, fly with us on your backs."

"Well, I have never heard of such a thing," Gertie said. "Have you, Sadie?"

"I didn't even think mice could fly," Sadie said.

"Now, let me try to explain," Edward said. "We can't fly. That is why we need you two. You will fly us north and we will ride on your backs." Edward stamped his paw and stared from one turkey to the other.

"That one is a bit grumpy," Sadie said to Nicholas.

"He's all right. It is just that we are in a bit of a hurry," Nicholas said. "What do you say?"

"We will be happy to take you," Sadie said.

"First thing in the morning," Gertie added. Both turkeys bobbed their heads.

"That's right," Sadie said. "I almost forgot. We don't fly in the dark."

"Now, don't go away," Gertie said to Nicholas and Edward. "We will be roosting in the trees right over there." She pointed with her outstretched wings. "In the morning we will be happy to take you south."

"Not south, north," Edward shouted to the birds as they fluttered up into the branches of a nearby pine tree. There was nothing left for Nicholas and Edward to do that night but sleep tucked into the stone wall. Nicholas tossed and turned all night, worrying that come morning the turkeys would have forgotten all about them.

True to their word, the two turkeys carried Nicholas and Edward north. They flew short distances through the woods and fields of Vermont. From St. Johnsbury the birds flew into the Northeast Kingdom.

The turkeys hadn't been this far north before, so for them it was an adventure. They liked to stop in the many lakes of the area. They flew up and over the rolling landscape. They walked under the green leaves of the oak, maple, and beech trees. Painted trillium blossomed in the woods and day lilies bobbed in the open sunshine. It was a beautiful time to travel in the state.

As the days passed, Nicholas learned to enjoy the rambling stories of the turkeys. Despite their forgetfulness, the wild birds knew a great deal of state history. "You would not believe it if I told you," Sadie said one day as they were all snacking on some beechnuts. "This whole part of the state was once covered with ice."

"She's right," Gertie added. "I've been told the ice was more than a mile thick and covered most of Vermont."

"That's right, Gertie," Sadie said. "Stories passed down in my family say that, after the ice, an ocean covered part of the state. Can you imagine, Gertie? We aren't much for swimming, are we?"

"I should say not," Gertie said. "Anyway, that was long before natives lived in the state."

"We've learned there were many native nations throughout New England," Nicholas said. "They tell their stories to each new generation. My family kept all their stories in a journal. That is why I am searching for my cousin Francis. He has our family journal."

"Nicholas and I have traveled all over New England chasing that journal. It is my hope we will find Francis and the journal right here in Vermont."

"My family has spread out all over New England. We only have the journal to keep the stories," Nicholas said.

"Gertie and I never tire of telling old stories to each other. Somehow they seem new each time we hear them."

"Yes, I am sure they do," Edward said. "My family has been in New England for as long as anyone can remember."

"So has ours," Sadie said brightly. "Do you suppose we are related?"

"Oh, I doubt that very much," Edward said.

"Yes, I am sure we are not," Gertie said. "You're a bit small to be a wild turkey."

"I may be small," Edward said, "but I have a few

stories of my own. Nicholas, tell them about the time I fought off a pack of wild weasels. I have told that story many times."

"Now Edward," Nicholas said, "I am sure these turkeys don't want to hear about your exploits in Maine."

The two turkeys listened as Edward went on at great length about how he foiled the weasels' plans to attack a colony of city mice in Bangor, Maine. By the time the story was over, it was time to move on again. The turkeys wanted to make one more flight north then return to the south. They were near a great lake called Memphremagog.

There was something about the lake that made the turkeys uneasy. They had heard stories about the lake. Animals they met along the way north had told them strange tales about something living in the deep water. Sadie and Gertie decided not to share these stories with Nicholas and Edward. They would find out soon enough.

Chapter Eight

Nicholas and Edward looked out over the long lake called Memphremagog. The summer sun sparkled on the water. Because of the islands and peninsulas jutting out on each side, it was hard for the small animals to see far up the lake.

"This is the very top of the state," Nicholas said. He was disappointed they had come all this way without any sign of his cousin.

The two turkeys sipped water from the lake. They stretched out their long necks and let the water run down their throats. Sadie looked out at the water. Small waves rolled along the surface. They washed up with a splash onto the rocky shore.

"How do you do? How do you do? A pretty day to be on the shore, that is for sure!" a small fuzzy animal next to the turkeys said.

Sadie jumped in the air and almost fell into the water. "Oh, my," she said, "I didn't see you there. Where did you come from?"

"You're standing right next to my home," the muskrat said. "I thought you had come for a visit. My name is Milton. I don't get very many visitors."

"We didn't know you lived here, but we are happy to meet you," Nicholas said. "My friend Edward and I are looking for my cousin Francis."

"You don't say," Milton said. "I have a cousin myself. He lives up the lake." Milton leaned in next to the animals and added, "He lives in Canada, you know. Wild place up there."

The two turkeys moved in close to hear the muskrat.

"My cousin is a small mouse like me. Maybe you have seen him?" Nicholas said. "He's carrying our family journal."

"No," Milton paused for a minute. "I can't say that I have. Small animals don't seem to stick around long."

Nicholas and Edward moved close to the low-talking muskrat. "It is so beautiful here," Nicholas said. "Why wouldn't small animals want to live here?" They all looked up at the mountains circling the lake, the fields of bright green grass rolling down to the water, and the clumps of trees growing along the hillsides.

"No, they don't seem to stick around long."

"Why is it that no one wants to spend much time here?" Edward asked.

"I'll tell you why," Milton said as he sat hunched over

amid the circle of animals. "It's on account of Memphre." Milton looked at the four animals. The turkeys looked at each other. Nicholas and Edward looked at the turkeys.

"I must say, I have never heard of this Memphre, whatever it is," Sadie said.

"Neither have I," Gertie said. "It doesn't sound too terrifying."

"Really now," Edward spoke up. "I don't know what all the fuss is about. I have faced down many a challenge in my time, have I not, Nicholas? I am sure that whatever this Memphre character is, I can handle it."

"That's right. Are you sure you haven't seen Nicholas's cousin?" Sadie said.

"No, no, no," Milton shouted. Everyone stepped back, breaking up the circle. "I'm trying to tell you there are no small animals around here because of the monster that lives in the lake," Milton shouted and pointed toward the calm water.

The turkeys gobbled and fluttered their wings. Nicholas and Edward jumped back, expecting the monster to appear out of the water.

"Hold on just a moment," Edward said. "You never said anything about this Memphre being a monster. You can't expect me to do anything about a lake monster."

"Ha," Milton said, "I frightened you all pretty good." The muskrat chuckled to himself at the expense of these animals from down south. "Now don't get all excited. This monster isn't the scary kind. I have never heard of him hurting anyone. To tell you the truth, I think he is kind of lonely."

"He must have lots of friends if he has lived on this lake for so long," Nicholas said.

"There's the thing, every time he tries to meet new friends his size kind of scares away animals. It has gotten so there are no animals in this area living close to the water."

"What about the mouse who came through here?" Nicholas asked. "Was he scared of Memphre? What ever happened to the mouse?"

"I'll tell you what," Milton said. "If you four can stay and meet Memphre, I know he will like you. It will make him so happy to talk with someone new. He usually shows up just before the sun goes down. Then, I will tell you all about a mouse who came through here."

"Well, I don't know if we can take the time to meet this monster of yours," Edward said.

"We agree with Edward," Sadie said.

Gertie bobbed her head also. "We agreed to bring you north, not do battle with any lake monsters."

"I don't know about the rest of you," Nicholas said, "but I think we should stay and visit with Memphre. He sounds very sad. I think we can help him. I know I need my friends to help me from time to time."

"Well, Nicholas," Edward said, "if you are going to stay, then I guess I better stay to help you, in case you run into trouble."

Chapter Nine

Milton the muskrat brought the animals up the east side of the lake. "I know somewhere quiet," Milton said as they scurried through the tall grass near the lakeshore. "Memphre doesn't like to come out where there are a lot of people."

"I don't know about all this," Sadie said. She walked along cautiously, putting down one claw after the other as if the monster were hiding in the grass.

"Now, there is no need to be nervous," Edward said. "Why, I would lead the way if Milton weren't already doing it." As he talked, he moved along more and more slowly, until he was the last animal in line.

Nicholas wanted to know more about the lake monster.

"He really doesn't like to be called a monster at all," Milton said. "I would say I know him about as well as anyone."

"If he is not a monster, then what is he?" Nicholas asked.

"Well, it is always nearly dark when I see him, so it is hard for me to say," Milton said. "There is one thing I know, I have never seen him out of the water. You don't have to worry about running into him in the grass, Sadie."

"Maybe his family came into the lake from the sea," Nicholas offered. "Maybe the lake monster, I mean, Memphre, is really looking for a way to get back to the sea."

"That could be," Milton said. "That could be, Nicholas. Maybe you can ask him if we see him. Now, we have a ways to go if we are going to get to the right spot before it gets too dark." The muskrat picked up the pace a bit.

Eventually, they came to just the right spot. The distant mountains, the clear blue lake water, and the green near shore framed a picture as beautiful as any Nicholas and Edward had ever seen. The sun, now a bright orange ball, was going down behind Owl's Head Mountain.

Sadie and Gertie scratched the ground, looking for something to eat. They slowly wandered up the hill away from the water. Nicholas sat on a hillock of grass and looked out at the water.

Edward settled into the tall grass, warmed by the day's sunshine. "I think this is an excellent chance to catch up on my rest," he said and promptly fell asleep, gently snoring as he dreamed.

"I will be back soon," Milton said. "I have a burrow nearby that I should check on while I'm in the neighborhood. I haven't been this far up the lake in some time. I won't be long," he added as he scampered off. The sun dropped down in the sky.

After the long walk up the lake, Nicholas felt sleepy. He didn't want to miss a chance to see Memphre, but he struggled to keep his eyes open. He fidgeted in the dry grass. Before long, his eyes blinked once, then twice. His head bobbed down. He was fast asleep. Nicholas dreamed of his parents. In his dream, they were calling him in for dinner and it was starting to rain.

He awoke to water splashing on him. Suddenly, he was wide-awake. It was nearly dark. The blue lake water was as calm as a mirror and looked black in the low light. Except for Edward who still slept nearby, Nicholas was alone. Out of the still water rose an animal that Nicholas did not recognize.

"Eiyee!" Nicholas shouted. He jumped off the hillock and ran around behind it. He peeked through the grass. The animal that looked somewhat like a seal and somewhat like a big snake bobbed in the water looking back at Nicholas. The animal sniffed once or twice.

"Who's there?" the animal asked. "I can smell you in the grass, but I can't see you."

"I am Nicholas. Are you going to hurt me?"

"What are you doing up here? I haven't seen any animals around here for some time."

"I am with Milton. He has brought me to find Memphre," Nicholas said.

"That's me," the animal said brightly. He bobbed up and down and splashed his head in the water. "I'm Memphre, or that's what I am called around here. Do you know Milton the muskrat?"

"He brought us here to see you," Nicholas said. "He said you know a lot about the history of this lake and the state."

"My family has lived in this lake for many years. We were here before anyone. We keep to the deep, dark water, but I like to come to the surface to see what is happening. Mostly, I think I frighten animals so I don't have many friends."

Nicholas sat down again on the lump of grass. "Tell me about this lake," he said.

Memphre was just happy that someone wanted to listen to him and not run away. He started talking about the great sheet of ice that covered most of the state. He included the coming of the native people, and didn't stop until he talked about the arrival of Europeans just a few short hundred years ago.

Nicholas was so interested that he forgot about everyone else. He would have been content to sit and listen to Memphre talk for hours if it weren't for the yell he heard coming out of the darkness.

Chapter Ten

In the moment Nicholas heard the scream, Memphre slipped below the surface of the water. Nicholas turned toward the sound. Edward awoke and jumped up. Milton came scurrying along the shore from the opposite direction.

"Oh, my, oh, my," Sadie was saying in the dark, "I saw him. I just saw him right there," she pointed with her beak at the water. "Did you see that hideous beast?"

Sadie said, as she came into view from the dark. Gertie trailed behind, cackling and clucking.

"Oh, yes," Gertie said, "I saw the monster. He was just about to attack Nicholas when we came along. Isn't that right, Sadie?"

"I am almost certain that is what was happening," Sadie said. "Oh, it was an awful sight."

"Now ladies, really," Edward said. "I was here the whole time. I had Nicholas protected from any harm. Isn't that right, Nicholas?"

"Memphre wasn't trying to harm me. He was telling me all about the history of the state."

"He was here?" Milton said. He finally made his way up from the lakeshore to where the others were standing. "What did I tell you, Nicholas? I told you he was all right. He just needs someone to talk to now and again."

"Well, from where we stood, it looked like he was about to eat you up," Sadie said. Gertie tried to back up her sister, but Edward interrupted.

"Do you think Memphre saw Francis?" Edward asked in a hurry. "Do you suppose we are close to catching up with him? Again?" Edward added.

"I am sure of it. He was about to tell me of a mouse he knows, who lives not too far from here, who may know a thing or two about our journal," Nicholas said.

"If that is the case, we must press on," Edward said.

"You have been so good to travel with me all this way, Edward. I couldn't have asked for a better friend. But we aren't done yet."

"There you go, Nicholas, getting all mushy on me. Hmmm," Edward said, clearing his throat. "I have said I will see you through this and I will. Now, which way should we head from here? There doesn't appear to be much more Vermont in this direction," Edward pointed up the dark lake.

"You're right about that," Milton said. "What did Memphre say about that mouse he saw a while back?"

"He said the mouse only stopped for one night. The mouse was on his way back to his barn, west of here. I think he was about to tell me more when we heard that scream." Nicholas looked at Sadie. The turkey busied herself grooming her feathers.

"That's all right, old girl," Milton said. "You couldn't help yourself, I'm sure. Now Nicholas, are you sure Memphre said the mouse was going west from here? It is rugged traveling for a small mouse such as yourself."

"Yes, he definitely said the mouse was going back west. He said he was headed to the barn where he lives," Nicholas said. "Maybe it was Francis. We won't know until we find that barn."

"How on earth are you going to find the right one? Do you have any idea how many old barns there are in this part of the state?" Milton asked.

Sadie and Gertie were staying quiet. They tried not to look at Nicholas or Edward. They were thinking it was well past the time for them to be looking for a tree to roost in for the night.

"We need to find a way to cover a lot of ground at

once," Nicholas said. He looked over at the turkeys that were trying to look very tired. "Don't worry, ladies. I wasn't thinking of you. I know you are out of your range as it is."

"Well, you see," Sadie said, "it isn't as though we wouldn't love to help."

"That's right," Gertie said "We would love to help, but we just don't travel in this area very often."

"And, there is that monster from the lake," Sadie said.

"That's right," Gertie added. "There is the monster. And, who knows what else lives up here so close to the border and all."

"Now let me think," Milton was saying. "You boys need to cover a lot of territory and be able to check out every barn you come across."

"That's right," Nicholas said. "I don't think flying will help with all the barns we have to check out. We need to stay low to the ground."

"Now, that makes sense to me," Edward added. He never was one for flying anyway. "I say we need to be able to trot along at a leisurely pace."

"I think you've hit on it," Milton suddenly said. "I know just the fellow to help you out. He loves to run tirelessly, knows this area inside and out, and, best of all, he can sniff out any little mice hiding in the big barns."

"You all stay here," Milton said. "I'll be back by morning with your ride."

Chapter Eleven

After the excitement of the long day, Nicholas and Edward slept late. They woke to the sound of a dog barking.

"What is all that noise?" Edward asked, as he rolled over to cover his ears.

Nicholas sat up and looked out over the meadow. A dog with long white fur bounded toward them. Milton waddled along behind, trying to keep up as best as his short legs would allow.

The dog made his way to Nicholas and Edward. "Woof, woof, woof! How do you do?" the dog said. His pink tongue hung out of his mouth as he panted. He looked at them with one blue eye and one gray eye. "There is nothing like a morning run to get the blood moving."

"We're fine. A bit tired I would say," Edward said. He rubbed his eyes with his paws. Milton was just now catching up with the dog. He huffed and puffed a bit.

"I see you have all met," Milton said. "This young husky is my dear friend Daniel. Daniel, these are the animals I was telling you about. What do you say, can you help them out?"

"These two little fellows? Why, they won't feel any heavier than the first November snowflakes."

"My friend Daniel is a sled dog. Well, sometimes he works as a sled dog. He's a bit independent minded," Milton said.

"Sometimes, especially in the spring and summer when there are no sleds to pull, I like to roam about the state. I see the sights. I learn what I can about this beautiful land. Keeps me in shape for the pulling season," Daniel said.

"That's why he will be the perfect guide for you two," Milton said. "Now you better get along while there is still a lot of daylight."

"Daniel, you must want to rest a while," Nicholas said. "It looks like you have come a long way already."

"Nonsense, I love to run," Daniel said. The dog bowed down for Nicholas and Edward. They scrambled up and made themselves comfortable in the husky's soft fur. Milton waved to the dog as he bounded away. When the husky was just a white speck on the field of green beside the lake, Sadie and Gertie landed near Milton.

"Have we missed anything? I slept so soundly," Sadie said. Gertie shook out her feathers and began scratching the ground for something for breakfast.

Daniel made a good companion for Nicholas and Edward. He knew his way around and he could run for hours. Nicholas and Edward told him they wanted to head west. Daniel kept the distant Jay Peak in front of him and trotted along from field to farm. A winding road, paved but potholed, wandered generally west.

"Now you must remember," Daniel said, "there are about as many barns in the state of Vermont as there are valleys to put them in. It may take some time to check each one for just the right mouse."

The first day the three animals sniffed out one barn after another. Some were in better shape than others. Some had cows inside. Some had pigs or sheep. One barn was full of old sleighs that could be pulled by horses. All of them needed paint.

"Phew, that was a bit smelly," Edward said. He was carefully stepping out of an old chicken barn. He had white feathers stuck in his fur.

Daniel, waiting outside, lapped up some water in a tin bucket and scooped up the dirty chipmunk. "You can never tell from the outside what you will find in an old barn," Daniel laughed. "Even a chipmunk with feathers."

"Well, I can tell you there was only a flock of angry chickens in that one," Edward said. He spit a small feather out of his mouth.

"No mice?" Nicholas asked. "No one who has heard of Francis?"

"I am afraid I couldn't even ask about Francis,"

Edward said. "Those chickens are too busy laying eggs to talk with me."

"Come on," Daniel said, "there are plenty more barns around here." The dog trotted on down the road.

Nicholas watched Jay Peak getting closer. They had turned off the main road and they followed a dirt track into the hills. There were few farms out here. The sun was sinking behind the mountains to the west.

As Daniel jogged along the road, Nicholas noticed an old barn ahead. At first he was excited to see it. Soon he saw half the roof had caved in, the big door swung loose in the breeze, and an old tractor, orange with rust, leaned to one side in the barnyard. "I don't think anyone could live in an old broken-down barn like this," Nicholas said.

"We better have a look," Daniel said. "You can't judge a barn by its boards, my old pop used to say."

Daniel turned in the driveway and picked his way around old tractor parts and clumps of rotting hay. A pair of barn swallows swooped out of the hole in the roof. An orange-and-white cat, with scars on his face and burrs in his fur, leapt out from behind a rusted red wheelbarrow and ran away from Daniel.

The husky couldn't help himself. Seeing the running cat, Daniel took off, spilling Nicholas and Edward on the ground. The cat ran around the corner of the barn and Daniel followed. Nicholas and Edward stood in the dirt.

"We will never catch up with Daniel," Edward said. "We might as well check out this barn."

It wasn't hard to find an opening into the rundown building. Nicholas and Edward peeked into the dimly lit building. Without warning, a fuzzy little mouse head looked out from inside the barn.

"Hello, Nicholas. I heard you were in the area."

Chapter Twelve

Nicholas jumped back away from the opening. He bumped into Edward, who was standing right behind him, and they both tumbled to the ground. The two animals tried to untangle themselves from each other. They rolled around on the dry, dusty ground. A cloud of dirt rolled up and into the barn.

From inside the barn, the mouse started coughing and waving his paws around. "I see some things never change," the strange mouse said. "When I left home, you were just a tiny mouse crawling around the ground and here you are still rolling around in the dirt."

Nicholas stood up and tried to brush the dust out of his fur. He thought he recognized the voice from somewhere.

Edward, choking and coughing, tried to pull himself upright, holding onto Nicholas's paw.

"Wait a minute, Edward. I think I know who that mouse is. It can't be though, can it?"

"I didn't think you would remember, Nicholas. It is me, Clarence, your big brother," the mouse said. He stepped out of the hole in the barn.

The dust settled and Nicholas could clearly see Clarence, who said, "I haven't seen you since you were a baby mouse, back on the farm."

"I do remember you," Nicholas said. "You used to let me chase your tail around our mouse house."

"That's right, and do you remember all the times I gave you part of my supper? You had such a big appetite," Clarence said. The two mice laughed over the memories.

Edward, standing by, cleared his throat.

"Oh, Clarence, this is my friend Edward," Nicholas said. "We have been traveling all over New England together." Edward bowed and introduced himself.

"So Nicholas, have you been at home recently? How are Mom and Dad? I have been hearing strange rumors about them. Tell me, what is going on back home?"

"Well, I haven't been home for over a year now. When I left, Mom and Dad were trying to rebuild our home after a big flood." Nicholas went on to explain to his brother all about getting washed out of their home. He told Clarence about their family journal that had been ruined and his long journey looking for the other copy to bring home for his family.

"I remember that journal. Dad would bring it out once in a while to write in it. He read some stories to us, too. I never thought about it too much," Clarence said. "There is a copy of the journal somewhere?"

Nicholas told his brother about Uncle William, who had the copy for a while and their cousin Francis, who was in the state of Vermont somewhere right now. "He has the only other copy of our journal. I promised Mom and Dad I would bring it home for us to make a new copy." After all the talking, Nicholas sat down in the dust again. Going over all that history made him tired.

"Don't sit out here in the dust," Clarence said. "Come on in. This barn may look a bit shabby on the outside but I have my home fixed up quite nicely." Clarence led Nicholas and Edward into the old barn. "I hope you are hungry," Clarence said. "I have stockpiles of food enough for all of us."

"Now that you mention it, I could use a bit of food," Edward said.

"What about Daniel?" Nicholas said. "We should tell him where we're going."

"If Daniel is the dog who is chasing Carmen, she will keep him occupied for a while. We will look for him after we eat. This farm was once a big apple orchard. I think you'll like what we have for dinner."

Inside the barn, Nicholas and Edward stopped and stared. There were stacks and stacks of apple crates.

All the apples had dried up to a wrinkled fraction of their old size, but to these small animals this was a feast. The hungry animals went from crate to crate sampling the different types of apples. There were Cortlands and McIntosh. There were Northern Spys and some old Crispin.

After they had eaten their fill, Clarence asked Nicholas where he was headed next.

"I have no idea where to look for Francis. We know he is looking for someone to help him with the journal.

We don't know who he is looking for or where he is going."

"Vermont may not be the biggest state in New England but, if you count all the mountains and hills, there is still a lot of ground to cover."

"Francis has more or less disappeared," Edward said. "We were all traveling together but we had a bit of an accident on a river and we haven't seen him since."

"Well, I came to Vermont because I like the peace and quiet up here but, I'll tell you what, Nicholas, I'll travel with you for a while. I know a few places Francis might be headed. It will do me some good to get off this farm for a while." Clarence tapped his overfull belly.

"Oh, that would be wonderful," Nicholas said. "We have been slowly heading west, searching all the barns we can find looking for Francis. Instead, we ran into you."

"There are too many barns to keep searching this way," Clarence said. "I think we should head directly to the western side of the state. But first, we have to find Daniel."

Chapter Thirteen

Carmen was a tough old barn cat. Most of the farm animals kept their distance. If they didn't, Carmen chased them away. Daniel, naturally friendly, could easily outrun the shaggy cat. Chuckling to himself, he sped out of the barnyard, up the hill toward the trees. He sat in the shade panting. He smiled, thinking of his fun. Carmen sauntered away, convinced she had seen the last of the dog.

Clarence led Nicholas and Edward out of the barn into the bright sunshine. They looked toward the rundown house. A rust red roof drooped across the sagging building. Clarence knew that Carmen steered clear of the man living alone inside.

"Follow me," Clarence said. "We have to check on our ride, then we can find Daniel. There are always out-buildings on these old Vermont farms," Clarence said. "There are plenty of places for a clever mouse to live."

"What are we looking for?" Nicholas asked. He ran alongside his older brother. It felt good to have him to rely on.

"You'll see, little brother," Clarence said. "We are going to travel west in style."

"Travel in style, you say?" Edward inquired. "Now we are talking about my kind of travel."

Clarence led Nicholas and Edward to a small build-ing that stood by itself. One of the three bay doors leaned over, hanging on one hinge. Inside the second bay, secured by its own closed doors, stood a shiny, red sports car. The car boasted big knobby tires, two open seats, and a long gleaming hood.

"The only thing the man in the house cares about on this farm is his antique car," Clarence said. "The barn is falling down, the house needs paint, but his sportster will roar to life at the turn of the key."

"How will we ever drive this car?" Nicholas said.

"Don't you worry, Nicholas," Clarence said. "The man in the house will be out soon. He likes nothing better than to roar up and down the country roads around here. And, because it is Friday, he will want to go on a long road trip. We just have to wait in the car and soon enough the man will be out."

Clarence was about to lead the others up and into the back seat of the car when Carmen appeared in the doorway.

"Aha," she said. "There you are, Clarence. I thought I chased you off this farm last week." Clarence turned and looked at the old cat.

"Hello, Carmen. I thought you were out dancing with young Daniel. Did you manage to catch him?"

Carmen didn't like to be reminded she was getting to be an old cat. She leapt at Clarence, who took off dragging Nicholas and Edward with him.

"Come on, Nicholas, this way!" Clarence said. The mice and the chipmunk scampered out to the barnyard.

"Ha, ha," Carmen said. "I may be getting old but I will catch up with your little legs."

The mice moved as fast as they could. Clarence veered off course toward an old water pump. He ran up the pump and out on the handle. Nicholas followed closely behind.

The cat stopped and sat under the pump, twitching her tail and smiling. "Well now," Carmen said, "it seems you have run out of places to run." She watched Nicholas sit beside his brother. Edward, a little plumper and a little slower, followed after them. He finally reached the end of the handle.

"What are we going to do?" Nicholas said. "We can't sit out here forever."

"That's right," Carmen said, "and when you get tired of your perch, I'll be right here."

The slap of a screen door closing on the porch made the animals look. "The man is leaving the house," Clarence said.

"He's heading for his car," Nicholas said. "We have to get back there."

Carmen just sat smiling, looking up at the pump. They all heard a high squeak. The animals on the handle felt it slowly sinking.

"The weight of all three of us is too much for the handle," Clarence said.

"I hope you are not looking at me," Edward said.

Now they heard the car engine roar to life. "Clarence, there goes the car," Nicholas said. "We have to do something."

The pump handle plunged down faster now. Carmen flicked her tail in the dirt, thinking she would have quite a dinner tonight. She opened her mouth to say something, when suddenly the pump gushed out a big splash of water. The cat yowled, leapt in the air, and took off shaking her tail and each leg in turn.

The other animals didn't have time to laugh over their good fortune. The shiny red car was backing out of the barn and turning toward the road.

"Oh, no," Nicholas said. "It is too late, we will never catch the car." They ran as fast as they could. The tailpipe of the roadster belched smoke as the driver shifted gears.

They were about to give up on the idea of the car ride when they heard barking. Daniel bounded up to them. "Climb aboard, I can catch that car. We don't have any time to waste."

Nicholas, Clarence, and Edward stood on the husky's head as he charged after the car. As the auto paused to avoid a deep pothole at the end of the drive, Daniel made a leap for the bumper. "Jump now," Daniel said. All three animals knew what to do and grabbed the shiny chrome bumper as the car sped off.

"Thank you, Daniel," Nicholas waved to the husky as he trotted back into the barnyard. He had taken a liking to that cat. Maybe we can be friends, Daniel thought to himself, sniffing the ground looking for Carmen.

Chapter Fourteen

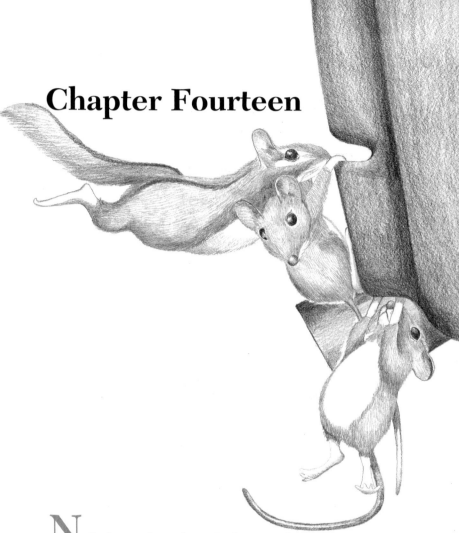

Nicholas, Edward, and Clarence held on to the shiny bumper of the speeding roadster. The driver, unaware of the animals hitching a ride, motored with abandon over the rolling road. The engine roared and the exhaust flew out the long tailpipe. The driver cackled with glee at every turn and dip in the road.

"Are you sure this is safe?" Edward shouted. "I thought we were going to travel in style."

"What better way to travel through the countryside than on the back of this classic car?" Clarence shouted back. He had a wide grin on his face and his tail whipped out in the breeze.

"If we manage to hold on," Nicholas said, "we will cover a lot of territory, but how will we get off this bumper?"

"Don't worry, Nicholas," Clarence said. "I've traveled this way many times. Sooner or later, the driver will get tired and hungry and want to stop."

The animals gritted their teeth and gripped the back of the car. The road wound back and forth as it climbed higher and higher into the Green Mountains. Gradually, the road flattened out as the car settled into the Champlain Valley.

"It won't be long now," Clarence said. Other cars appeared on the road. "We will be going by the Missisquoi National Wildlife Refuge soon. We could spend weeks there. There are all sorts of birds and animals I could introduce you to, Nicholas."

"Maybe those animals know of our cousin," Nicholas said.

"Oh, I don't think so," Clarence said. "Many of the birds are migratory. They come for a season, but they always move on. If I know this driver, we're headed for Lake Champlain. I know someone there who can help us. I am sure of it."

"I do hope so," Edward replied. "It is getting a bit chilly riding on the back of this old car. And, what about something to eat soon? It seems ages since we have eaten."

"Just be patient, Edward," Clarence said. "When we stop, we'll eat and find my old friend."

The car continued past Missisquoi and headed for Champlain. The sun was in the western sky now. The hills and mountains of New York State stood on the far shore.

"There is a string of islands that runs down this lake," Clarence said. "We're almost there."

The car traveled slowly now on a narrow road. The animals could see the lake in the distance beyond farm fields. Summer cottages nestled among the trees near the shore. Old farmhouses stood back from the water at the edge of waving cornfields. The car stopped in front of a small motel, really just two or three rooms and an office.

"Here we are," Clarence said. "Quick, hop off the car! We only have a moment."

Nicholas and Edward followed Clarence away from the car and ran behind the motel building. A line of birch trees shaded the building from the late day sun. Clarence ran between the trees and out to the edge of the lake.

It was getting dark on the east side of the island. The waves lapped at the shore. The animals climbed up and over the jumble of rocks. Clarence held his head up now and then to sniff the cool air. He peered into the trees from time to time. "He must be around here, somewhere," Clarence said in a whisper.

From high in the sky came a piercing screech. All the animals froze at once.

"Ahh, what is that?" Nicholas asked. He hunkered down in the rocks.

Edward dove under a stone, chittering to himself.

But Clarence looked up into the darkening sky and pointed. "There he is," Clarence said. "I knew we would find him. He'll help us find Francis."

As Clarence talked, a great bird with crooked wings and a sharp beak swooped down and landed on a tree branch. With a fluttering of wings, the bird gripped the branch and turned his eye toward the ground.

"Clarence, is that you?" the osprey asked. "Who is that with you, hiding among the rocks?"

"It's me, Clarence. I have brought my youngest brother to meet you. His friend Edward is down here somewhere."

"I'm right here," Edward said. "I must have slipped on these wet rocks." Edward tried to scuff the stones with his paws.

"Hello there," Nicholas said. "My brother said you might be able to help us find our cousin."

The osprey settled his feathers and flexed his talons on the tree branch. He stared down at the animals on the shore. Just as Nicholas was beginning to think the bird was not going to respond to him, he said, "I have no time to track the whereabouts of a small mouse. I am Ethan. I am named after the most famous Vermonter in history."

"I have learned that we all can make history. We are all part of one big story that goes back as far as we can remember," Nicholas said. "And our story will go on after us."

"That's what Nicholas is trying to tell you," Clarence said. "Our cousin Francis is working to learn about his past. He is in Vermont and you know so much about Vermont. Maybe you can help us?"

Ethan, the osprey, stood up tall on his legs, flapping his wings as if he were going to take off. Nicholas thought his last chance to find his cousin would fly off with the osprey. Instead, the osprey flew down to the lowest branch on the tree. The branch hung out over the lake and bobbed with the weight of the bird.

"I will help you," Ethan said. "But first, you must do something for me."

Chapter Fifteen

Nicholas sat up. He wanted to find out what the bird wanted from him. He hoped it would be something easy, such as bringing some sticks for a nest or maybe pulling a thorn out of his wing.

"Tell me," Clarence said "where is your friend Molly? I haven't seen her around the lake."

"That is it," Ethan said. "You must help me free her. She was caught and banded and put in a truck. I heard she is being taken to New York State, to a lake far away in the Adirondack Mountains."

"That sounds terrible," Nicholas said. "Why would they do that?"

"They want to bring osprey back to the lakes there, but she belongs here, with me," Ethan added.

"Now see here," Edward said, "I don't think we have time to chase after a caged osprey, Nicholas. We are having enough trouble catching up with one little mouse."

"That is the catch," Ethan said. "I will help you find your cousin if you help me save my friend Molly."

"We will do it," Nicholas said. "Won't we, Clarence?"

"I think it will be the fastest way for us to find Francis. So, I guess, yes, we will help you find Molly." Clarence stood next to his younger brother.

Edward sighed. He could see it was no use arguing with the two mice.

"Tell us," Edward said, "just how are we going to locate your friend Molly?"

"They were headed for the ferry to New York. It is just across the island from here," Ethan said. "You will have to hurry if you are going to catch the truck while it waits for the ferry."

"We will get there," Nicholas said. "Don't you worry, you will have to follow us in the air. We may need your help."

The three animals wanted to waste no time in heading for the far side of the island. Ethan swooped down low and landed in front of the animals. "Just wait a moment and I will be right back," Ethan said. He lifted off the ground again and flapped away into the dark. The animals on the ground could follow the bird as a black silhouette against the star-filled sky.

Ethan wasn't gone long before they heard him

return. He carried a stick in his talons from the nest he and Molly were building. "Here we go," he said, as he landed again. "Climb on. Even with the weight of all three of you, I will make faster time than you could on the ground."

Clarence and Nicholas sat on one end of the stick. Edward balanced them out by sitting on the opposite end. Ethan kept the stick pointed in the direction of his travel and took off. "I will carry you like I do a freshly caught fish," he said. "It is easier to fly this way."

Nicholas sneezed from the dust at takeoff. Clarence marveled at the millions of stars overhead. Edward wrapped his legs tightly around the small stick and let out a squeak. "Are you sure this is safe?" he asked the big bird.

"Why, I don't know," Ethan said. "I've never really done anything like this before." He flapped his wings and let out a screech that echoed off the water. The chain of islands at the top of Lake Champlain is long from north to south but narrow from east to west. It didn't take long for the fast-flying bird to cross over the fields and trees in the middle of the island. Ethan reached the far shore while it was still dark. He gently landed in a strip of grass near the ferry terminal.

The big ferry idled at the dock. Cars and trucks waited in a parking lot on shore to board the boat. Ethan left the animals in the grass and flew over the still cars. He called out to Molly as he flew. He circled down low over a white truck. A large canvas-covered

box filled the back. An answering screech came from under the canvas.

Ethan wheeled around and headed back for the animals hiding in the field. "I heard her," he said. "I heard her underneath the canvas."

Clarence and Nicholas stood up as high as they could and tried to see across the road. "She's on that truck, right there," Clarence said.

Edward marched right out and started across the road. He jumped back as a speeding car came squealing around a corner. It was the shiny red roadster from Clarence's farm. "He almost ran me over," Edward said. "Did anyone see that?"

"Edward, you have to be careful. We need a plan before we go running out into the road," Nicholas said.

Ethan flew back to the truck. He let Molly know he was here to help her. The three smaller animals remained huddled together. They started talking in low voices, trying to come up with a plan to rescue Molly.

Chapter Sixteen

Clarence, Nicholas, and Edward finished making their plans. They looked at one another before they

crept out into the road. The sun was coming up again on the far side of the island. They paused at the edge of the blacktop, then scurried as fast as they could across the road.

They noticed the red roadster loudly idling at the end of the line of vehicles waiting to board the morning ferry to New York. The driver of the car sat looking out over his windshield, impatiently drumming his fingers on the wooden steering wheel. He held a hot cup of coffee in his other hand. Steam rose above the cup into the cool air.

Before the animals on the ground made their move, they looked into the sky for Ethan. He continued to fly in a big lazy circle over the parking lot. He never took his eyes off the truck. A pair of seagulls, who made their home on the big lake, joined Ethan circling over the cars. The gulls counted on a bit of breakfast from the waiting drivers.

"Now, remember," Clarence said. "We have to time our jump right or else this won't work. We have to give Edward time to do his part."

Edward hesitated, then nodded.

Clarence said, "Come on, let's go, Nicholas. Edward, we'll see you soon." Clarence and Nicholas went toward the roadster. Edward made his way onto the white truck. He stood on top of the canvas-covered box. He found the box was really a cage. He clung to the bars on top and looked back toward the end of the line of cars.

Nicholas and Clarence were standing on the back of the red car. They hopped down into the back seat. The driver of the roadster opened a paper bag. He balanced the coffee between his knees. Nicholas could almost taste the blueberry muffin as the driver started to eat. The seagulls took notice of the paper bag from the air.

There was a blast from the ferry's horn. It was time to load the cars. The first few vehicles slowly rolled onto the deck of the boat. The driver of the roadster held his muffin in one hand and the coffee in the other. He let the car creep forward with the others. Clarence and Nicholas scrambled up to the back of the front seat.

The white truck and Molly were next to board. "Come on," Clarence said, "it's now or never." He jumped from the seat back down into the front seat. Nicholas followed right behind. At first the driver of the car didn't see the mice in his car. He was busy trying to eat and drive.

He took a bite of his muffin and dropped part of it on the seat. It landed next to the mice. The seagulls overhead saw the muffin fall and decided it was time to swoop and retrieve the morsel. The driver reached over for the muffin. He saw the mice and shrieked. The gulls squawked and dove into the car. The man waved at the birds and shrank down into the car. He saw the mice and jumped up in his seat. In his excitement, he stepped on the gas pedal. He tried to grab the steering wheel and spilled his coffee. The car gathered speed.

The driver, trying to shoo away the seagulls and stay away from the mice, swerved his car out of line. He headed straight for a small stream next to the ferry landing. He was too late in realizing what was about to happen. His shiny red car plunged over the low bank and into the stream. The mice hopped out of the car and ran for the white truck.

All activity stopped at the ferry. The workers came over to see what happened to the red car. Other drivers got out of their cars, offering suggestions on how to get the car out of the stream. The driver of the white truck stopped just before boarding the ferry to see what was going on. Edward saw his chance and worked away on the knots of the canvas cover.

"Who's out there?" Molly asked. She could hear Edward talking to himself.

"Don't worry about a thing," Edward whispered. "I'll have you out of there in a jiffy." He tugged this way and that on the line. It would not come free.

The excitement over the red car had died down. They continued to load the ferry. The white truck started up again and rolled forward.

Edward gnawed at the ropes. He wanted to get the canvas off and get off the ferry before it left for New York.

The white truck was the last vehicle to get on the boat. The big gate clanged shut. The ferry tooted its horn as the boat pulled away from the dock.

Edward could feel the boat moving. He took one last

nip at the rope and broke the knot. The line slipped free and the canvas top flapped off the cage.

Molly looked upward and saw Ethan in the sky. She leapt from her perch, through the open top and into the sky, letting out a cry. The two birds circled around each other and flew off toward the far end of the lake.

Ethan dipped his wings at the waving mice on the ground. They were happy for the two birds. They looked from the sky toward the ferry picking up speed as it left Vermont.

"Where is Edward," Nicholas asked. "I didn't see him get off the ferry."

On the ferry, Edward looked at the widening gap of water between him and the land. He looked for Nicholas and Clarence. Edward felt the breeze off the lake ruffle his fur. He was off to New York State and had no way of telling his friends where he was.

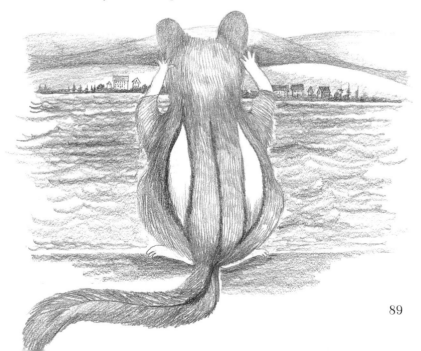

Chapter Seventeen

Ethan and his friend Molly cruised back up the lake. They flew wing tip-to-wing tip. Molly landed safely in a tree hanging over the lake. She didn't want to take a chance on ending up in a cage again. Ethan landed on a boulder near the shore. Nicholas and Clarence stood on the ground near a patch of red clover watching the birds.

"I have to thank you two. I couldn't have rescued Molly on my own," Ethan said. "Now, tell me, what is it I can do for you?"

"We are looking for my cousin Francis. He is somewhere in Vermont searching for information about our family history."

"Well, there is much history to learn about this state," Ethan said. "I myself am named after one of the Allen brothers who helped shape this state."

"I've heard all about Ethan and Ira Allen," Clarence said. "They helped to settle the boundary with New York and New Hampshire back at the beginning of our country, right?"

"That's right. Their group of Green Mountain boys protected Vermont and fought during the Revolutionary War," Ethan said. "Ethan Allen helped to found what is now one of Vermont's biggest cities—Burlington."

"We haven't looked in any cities for Francis," Nicholas said. "I just thought Francis would stay away from lots of people."

"Now, wait a minute," Ethan said. "Burlington is just the place to look for a mouse from away. There is plenty of history, food, and activity. He would be sure to find whatever he is looking for in Burlington. The more I think about it, the more correct it seems. You must head to Burlington."

"We'll do it," Clarence said. "I haven't been to Burlington since I passed through there when I moved to the state. I can show you the way, Nicholas."

"Molly and I must be off, too. We are going to spend the rest of the summer on the lake. She wants to fly south early this year. You know, get a jump on a winter home and all," Ethan said.

Ethan flew up to the tree where Molly waited.

"Good-bye, little mice," Molly said. "You have been most kind to help me. We won't forget you." She and Ethan lifted off the branch together and flew up high toward the thin white clouds streaking the blue sky over the lake.

Clarence said, "Nicholas, it is a long way for two little mice to get to Burlington. We better get started."

"What about Edward?" Nicholas said. "How are we going to let Edward know where we have gone?"

"All Edward has to do is stay on the ferry and he will come right back to the place where he started," Clarence said.

"It sounds easy, but sometimes Edward can be, well, a bit excitable," Nicholas said. "He might take a notion to get off the ferry and there is no telling where he will end up."

"As for the message, maybe those seagulls will look out for Edward," Clarence said. "I bet if we get them a bit of food they will help us."

"I don't know," Nicholas said. "They look a bit rough around the edges."

Clarence bounded off toward the birds. The two gulls were busy pecking at some trash left behind by the departing vehicles. Nicholas watched from a distance as his brother approached the gulls.

"Excuse me," Clarence said. "My brother and I need to ask you for a favor."

"Squawk, skree, skree," the first gull shrieked. Both birds flapped their long wings, lifting off the ground for only a moment. They landed again between the mice and their food.

"Who's that?" the gull asked. She flapped her wings, stretched her neck out, and squawked loudly. "Say, that's my dinner. You two look for your own."

"Now, now," the second gull said. "Don't mind her, she's a bit far-sighted. She can only see far off. It makes her a bit jumpy, you know."

"Oh, that's all right," Clarence said. "It would take more than an ornery gull to scare me off."

"Now see here, Nancy," the first gull said, "I am not jumpy. I am hungry. There's a difference, you know."

"Yes, Sydney, of course there is a difference. Now let's see what these nice little mice would like."

"I bet they would like a bite," Sydney said, snapping her beak toward Nicholas. Nicholas jumped back, even though he was nowhere near the gull's beak.

"There, there, young fella," Nancy said. "Don't mind Sydney. She would never hurt a mouse. Now would you, Syd?"

"Hmm, we'll see," Sydney said.

Nicholas thought he could see a twinkle in the gull's eyes so he dared to move closer to the big birds.

"We were wondering—" Nicholas said. "We need to get a message to a chipmunk friend of ours. He got stuck on the ferry. We hope he will be back soon. We need to tell him we have gone off to Burlington."

"Well, well," Sydney said. "You are in a bit of pickle. Speaking of food, how about you find us a tasty snack and, not only will we tell your friend where you have gone, but Nancy and I will take you to Burlington. What do you say to that?"

Nicholas looked at his brother. If they kept this up, they would be doing favors for every animal in the state of Vermont. On the other hand, they could cover a lot of ground if the gulls carried them to Burlington. The two mice shrugged.

"Okay," Nicholas sighed. "We'll do that for you. Just wait here. We'll be right back."

Chapter Eighteen

Nicholas and Clarence ran back over the parking lot, looking for something the gulls might have missed. The lot was empty now that the ferry was gone. Off to one side, a tractor had arrived to pull the red roadster out of the stream. The driver was trying to direct the operation from the stream bank.

Nicholas took advantage of all the confusion to make his way back into the red car. He found what was left of the driver's muffin and carried it over his head up from the floor of the car. He reached the top edge of the seat and called for Clarence to come help. "Clarence, catch this muffin!" He heaved the half a muffin over his head.

The driver saw the muffin come sailing out of the car and land on the ground near his feet. Clarence ran up, took the muffin in his paws, and scampered away as fast as he could go. Nicholas leapt out of the car and followed Clarence.

"I don't believe it," the driver said to no one in particular. "Those mice just stole my breakfast."

"Here you go, ladies," Nicholas said, laying the food at their webbed feet. "I hope you like your breakfast. It smelled good when it was still warm."

"We're not so fussy when it comes to food," Sydney said. "We like to eat and we don't mind where the food comes from." Sydney and Nancy pecked at the muffin. They argued over who would get the bits with blueberries. Nicholas and Clarence jumped out of the way while the birds ate.

When they were done, Sydney was about to fly off when Nancy spoke up. "Aren't you forgetting something, Sydney?" Nancy asked. "We promised these little mice a ride to Burlington."

"Don't forget we need you to look out for Edward when he comes back on the ferry," Nicholas said.

"He and I have come too far for me to lose him here."

"First things, first," Sydney said. "You two take your pick." She gestured with her wing tip at Nancy and herself. "Either of you can ride with either of us. It won't make much difference to us."

Nicholas climbed on Nancy's back and Clarence chose Sydney. The birds wasted no time and leapt into the sky. They cried out as they left the ground. The gulls liked to fly over the lake. Nicholas, who loved flying, leaned over each side trying to look out at the passing landscape. There were mountains all around the lake. Trees, in full summer green, covered the mountains and ran down to the water's edge.

The water was a pure blue, reflecting the color of the sky. A trail of white water marked the passage of boats traveling up and down the lake. A flock of cormorants flew in the opposite direction of the gulls. They were off for their morning's fishing. A graceful snowy egret flew up out of the reeds near the shore and traveled along the waters edge.

"What a magnificent lake," Nicholas said. "It must be wonderful to live here."

"Oh, it's all right, I guess," Nancy said slowly. Until this point Clarence had not said a word. He held tightly to Sydney's neck and flew along with his mouth open.

"You guess this is all right?" Clarence said. "Why, Nicholas, if I had known how wonderful it is to fly, I would have tried it long ago." He bounced up and down on Sydney's back. "Just look at," Clarence waved

one paw slowly, "everything," he ended. He didn't want to leave anything out.

"I am so glad you like to fly," Nicholas said. "Edward and I have flown together several times. He doesn't care for it so much." Clarence and Edward spent the rest of their flight pointing out sites to each other. They flew past North Hero and Grand Isle. When they passed South Hero, the gulls bent their course east toward the Vermont side of the lake.

"That must be Burlington," Clarence shouted. He pointed ahead to a large city built on the hills right next to the lake.

"Sit still now," Sydney said. "Landing is always the trickiest part." The two birds flapped their wings, glided for a bit, then set down on the water and glided to a stop in front of an aquarium.

"Here you are now," Nancy said. "This is Burlington."

"That's right," Sydney said. "We said we would get you here, now we have business of our own to attend to." The mice scrambled up some pilings near the aquarium and the gulls took off right away. "There is always some tasty fish left over from feeding time," Sydney said as the gulls wheeled by the mice.

"We don't want to miss it," Nancy said. "Good luck, little mice."

Nicholas and Clarence tried to say good-bye, but the birds were already focused on their next meal.

"Well," Nicholas said, "here we are." He looked up the hill. Block after block of city buildings marched down the hills toward the water. From where Nicholas and Clarence stood, the city of Burlington looked about as big as any city they had ever seen.

"I don't even know where to begin to look," Nicholas said. The two brothers, whiskers twitching and tails swaying, started up the hill and into the busy city.

Chapter Nineteen

Burlington's waterfront was a hectic place. Boats bobbed in the marinas. Visitors strolled through the parks near the shore. A sightseeing train rolled along the tracks leading away from the water.

"Look at all the people," Clarence said. "We don't get so many visitors where I live."

"Follow me," Nicholas said. "I have gotten used to dealing with crowds." He found a path away from the waterfront. He and Clarence headed for the blocks of brick buildings making up Burlington's downtown.

They ran across streets and around parked cars. They followed their noses and the smell of food in the air.

In no time they found themselves on Church Street. Standing near the top of the hill, they looked down on block after block of outdoor cafés and restaurants. Late-afternoon shoppers were settling in at the tables set out on the walkway. At one café after another, small white lights twinkled on, illuminating the area.

"Oh me, oh my," Clarence said. "Can you smell all that good food? It seems like ages since we ate."

"Come on," Nicholas said. "There must be food for mice like us behind all these restaurants. We might run into Francis looking for a meal." Nicholas led the way down an alley between two stores. A big blue dumpster held more food than the mice could ever eat.

"Help me up," Clarence said. "I am starving." The two mice ran around the back looking for a way into the dumpster.

It was dim in the narrow alley. The mice were more focused on finding a meal than looking out for anyone else. Clarence came to a halt in a confusion of black fur. Nicholas plowed right into him. The two mice sneezed and coughed and tried to untangle themselves from the black-furred animal.

"Slow down there, slow down," the animal said to the mice. He backed away and held one mouse in each of his own paws. "Who do we have here?"

"Hey, put us down," Clarence demanded. "We are sorry to have run into you but that is no reason to treat us so roughly." Nicholas and Clarence dangled from the skunk's paws.

"We are just so hungry we didn't see you," Nicholas said.

The skunk held him close to his face. He snuffed his narrow nose at the mouse. "Do I know you?" the skunk asked. "You sure look familiar." The skunk sat down on his tail. He kind of hunched over but didn't let go of the mice. "I'm Samuel."

"I don't think we have ever met," Nicholas said. "I have never been in Burlington before."

"Maybe it is Francis," Clarence said. "We came to Burlington looking for our cousin Francis, he kind of looks like Nicholas. Maybe you have seen him?"

The skunk twisted Nicholas one way then another trying to get a good look at the small mouse. "No, if I met a mouse named Francis, I think I would remember it," the skunk said.

Nicholas sighed and hung limply in the skunk's paws.

"Don't worry, Nicholas," Clarence said. "We'll find our cousin sooner or later. Just you wait."

"Say, ah, Sam, do you think you could put us down? We're very hungry and we really would like something to eat."

The skunk seemed to have forgotten that he was holding two mice in his paws. "Hey, what's that now? Oh, certainly, here you go. Don't call me Sam. I'm Samuel, named after the French explorer who gave his name to the big lake out there." The skunk set

Nicholas and Clarence on the cement and gestured to the lake. The mice rubbed their fur and frisked their whiskers a bit.

"You two kind of startled me, that's all. Let me help you." The skunk waddled over to the dumpster and gently picked up the mice again. He placed them in the side door. "Help yourselves. I've had plenty of good meals around here."

Nicholas and Clarence rummaged through the bags and boxes of old food. The skunk dipped his nose in and pulled out a half-eaten corncob. Nicholas dined on soft cherries and a crust of dark bread. Clarence, used to farm food, was overwhelmed with his choices. He sampled a little bit of everything.

"There now, that's better," Clarence said. He licked his lips and once again smoothed out his soiled whiskers.

"I was so hungry," Nicholas said. He continued to nibble on a cherry pit.

The skunk, busy with his own meal, popped his head up hearing the voices. "Who's there?" he asked. "Who's in my dumpster?"

Nicholas and Clarence sat up and waved their paws at the skunk. "It's just us," Nicholas said. "It's Clarence, and I'm Nicholas."

"Oh yes, oh yes," the skunk said. "Now I remember. Say, what are you two doing in my dumpster?"

Nicholas and Clarence hopped down out of the dumpster and looked at the skunk. "You know,"

Nicholas said. "You helped us in the dumpster so we could eat. We are looking for our cousin Francis."

"You two do look familiar," the skunk said. "Sometimes I forget things, but I never forget a face." Samuel started to waddle out of the alley. The mice followed behind. Samuel stopped at the edge of the shadows just out of view of the diners at the café. "Aha, I remember now," Samuel said. "I knew you two looked familiar."

"What did you remember," Nicholas asked. "Who do you think we look like?"

"I knew I would remember. Follow me," Samuel said. "There is someone nearby who has been searching for you."

Chapter Twenty

Nicholas tried to focus on following the skunk but he couldn't help thinking about whom Samuel was taking them to see. He hoped it was his cousin Francis. "Who else could it be?" he reasoned to himself. No one else knew he was in Vermont. He would like to find his cousin and get on with their journey.

Clarence followed behind the skunk. He knew it was dangerous to be so close to the back end of a skunk, but he didn't want to lose the dark animal in the shadows. Samuel stood on his hind legs a moment. He sniffed the night air. "I hope you don't mind, but we are going to take a short detour." He led Nicholas and

Clarence down a dimly lit side street. Nicholas felt uneasy heading away from the main crowd.

"Will this take long?" Nicholas asked. "What if we miss whoever is looking for me?"

Samuel didn't respond to the mouse. Occasionally he would stop to sniff the air, but otherwise he traveled along quietly in the dark. Clarence kept looking back behind them. The noise of the crowds was getting fainter.

At one point, Samuel picked up his pace a bit. His back end waddled from side-to-side as he moved. He turned down another side street and stopped. "Aha," he said, "I thought it was you." He rubbed noses with another skunk. She held her tail high in the air. "I must say," Samuel said, "I thought I caught a scent of you while I was up on Church Street."

Samuel was nodding and smiling as the other skunk talked. "I'm glad I found you, Samuel," the other skunk was saying. "Ben & Jerry's has a new flavor out. I think we should go try it."

"You don't say, Sandy," Samuel said. "I am always up for a little ice cream after dinner." Samuel and Sandy turned downhill heading for the ice-cream store. Nicholas and Clarence had no choice but to follow along. Nicholas was sure Samuel had forgotten all about them. "Sandy, we may need a little extra ice cream tonight, I have friends with me." Samuel gestured behind them toward the mice.

The skunks slowed down near the brightly lit

ice-cream shop. It was decorated with big paintings of black-and-white cows. People lined up inside tasting ice cream from small wooden spoons and sipping water from paper cups. The animals tried to stay in the shadows.

"I don't know about this," Nicholas said to Clarence.

"Oh, don't worry about anything," Samuel said. "Sandy is well known down here. If anyone can get some ice cream, she can." Sandy waddled slowly toward the store. She wandered back and forth, rubbing against a street sign that said Main Street.

Inside the store a small boy said, "Look Mommy, there's a kitty outside." The boy let go of his mother's hand and ran out to the sidewalk. Sandy let the boy lead her toward the store. Other customers looked over thinking they were seeing a stray cat. "The kitty has paint on her back," the little boy was saying. Sandy tried her best to purr.

"That's not a cat," one of the adults shouted from inside the store. The line of customers all turned toward the door. Everyone realized at once what they were looking at. "It's a skunk," two or three customers shouted at once. All the people inside the store tried to exit out the back hall at once. There was a great deal of shouting and shoving and grabbing up of loose children.

Sandy nodded her head at Samuel and the mice. They followed her as she calmly stepped inside the now-empty store.

The girl behind the counter smiled. "Why, hello there, Miss Skunk. We haven't seen you around here for a while." She scooped out three cups of the newest flavor and placed them on the floor.

Sandy and Samuel licked away at the softening ice cream. Nicholas and Clarence almost fell in their cup.

"Mmmm," Nicholas said, "it tastes like cake."

Samuel lifted his head. He had a mustache of ice cream on his furry face. "Cake," he said, ice cream dripping from his lip. "I nearly forgot. We were headed to find that fellow who has been looking for you." The customers, who had run around to the front of the store, were watching the animals through the window. As the skunks, Nicholas, and Clarence made for the door, the people stepped away.

"Good-bye, dear Sandy," Samuel said. "I will see you soon." He rubbed noses again with the other skunk. He gestured for the mice to follow him. Samuel did his best to waddle back up the hill. "There is a tiny shop on the corner of the street," he said. "They sell the most delicious cookies, bars, and cakes. I believe we will find the old fellow there."

The patrons went back inside Ben & Jerry's, shaking their heads in wonderment.

Chapter Twenty-One

By this time it was very late. Most of the cafés and restaurants were closed. The stars in the sky were fading into a blue-black sky. Animals used to being up all night were looking for a place to sleep. Samuel yawned as he waddled along. Nicholas and Clarence had been up all day and now all night. Wearily they stumbled up the hill following the old skunk.

"Well, I am off to find my bed," Samuel said to no one in particular.

Nicholas stopped in his tracks. "Wait just a minute," he said. "You said you would take us to someone who has been looking for me."

The tired skunk turned around and squinted at the little mouse. "Why are you following me? I am tired and need to get some sleep," Samuel said. He started to turn around.

Nicholas tugged on the skunk's tail. Clarence shuddered and covered his head with his paws. He knew what could happen when you fooled around with a skunk's tail.

Nicholas stood firm with his paws balled up. "You know who I am! I'm Nicholas and you said you knew someone who needed to talk with me. We were going there when you got sidetracked with the ice cream."

Samuel turned back to look at the mouse again. He held up his tail. Clarence dove under a stray napkin in the gutter. "Ice cream, you say?" Samuel said. He seemed to be thinking hard. "Sandy likes ice cream. We always go to Ben & Jerry's down the street. The counter girl is always so nice."

"That's right," Nicholas said. "We had ice cream, remember, then you were leading us to someone who knew me?"

Samuel was humming a bit and clicking his claws on

the pavement. "You know, little mouse, you certainly do remind me of someone."

"You said that before," Nicholas said. "When I mentioned cake, that reminded you of something." Nicholas nodded his head and beckoned toward Samuel with his paws. He tried to coax the memory out of the old skunk.

"Cake, that's it," Samuel shouted after a moment. "Why, we are nearly to the shop now. How silly of me. Of course I remember. Come along, I am frightfully tired."

Clarence flung the napkin off and followed Samuel and Nicholas. The three animals reached a crossroad to Church Street. A small glass building, with a single light on inside, stood in front of them. Nicholas watched a black lab, with a red bandana tied around his neck, sniff at the back door of the glass building.

The dog reminded Nicholas of the little black lab puppy he met on a fishing boat in Gloucester, Massachusetts. Then, he remembered where else he saw a black dog like that. When Nicholas ran up to the glass building, he could smell bread and cakes, freshly delivered, sitting on racks inside. He pressed his nose up against the glass. He pounded on the glass with his little paws.

"It is him," Nicholas said. "I can't believe he is here, so far from his home." Nicholas scampered around looking for a way into the building. Just as he went around one corner, he noticed a small chip in the glass near the sidewalk. A rather plump mouse was backing his way out of the hole. He dragged half a bagel with him.

"Uncle William, is that you?" Nicholas said. The old mouse straightened up, still holding the bagel in his paws. He looked bewildered for a moment. He dropped the pastry, jumped forward, and hugged Nicholas.

"Indeed," Uncle William said, "It is I." The two mice danced around, happy to have found one another. After a moment or two, Clarence walked up to the two happy mice. "I am Clarence, Uncle William. Nicholas has told me all about you."

Uncle William looked from Clarence to Nicholas

and back again. "Of course, Clarence. The last time I saw you, you were a tiny little mouse trying to run away from your mother."

All three mice laughed for a moment. Uncle William stopped suddenly and put his paw up to his head.

"What is it?" Nicholas said. "What is wrong?"

"Clarence, I am glad you are here, too," Uncle William said. "This concerns you as well."

"Tell us," Nicholas said.

William took a paw of each of the younger mice. "It is your parents," he said.

"Our parents," Nicholas shouted. "What is wrong? Are they all right? Where are they?"

"Well, you will not believe this, but they are right

here in Vermont," William said. "Now don't worry, they're all right. Well, not exactly, but they are fine."

"Uncle William," Clarence said, "please just tell us what is going on. Why are our parents in Vermont?"

"Now boys, listen and I will tell you everything, but not out here in the open." The mice looked around. The sun had come up and people passed by on their way to work. The black lab had been sniffing in the shadows. He picked up the scent of a skunk. Before the mice could warn him, he got a nose full from Samuel.

The dog ran off howling. Samuel grumbled to himself about nosey dogs and waddled off to his bed. The mice each grabbed a part of the fallen bagel and looked for a quiet place to pass the day and hear the news about their family.

Chapter Twenty-Two

Uncle William led his nephews out of the city to Battery Park, overlooking Lake Champlain. They found a safe place to hide and rest along a stone wall circling the park. They shared the bagel from the bakeshop. Nicholas now had a full belly. The late summer sun beat down on the three mice.

Clarence curled right up and went to sleep. Uncle William was nodding off sitting up. Nicholas tried to fight the urge to sleep. He blinked his eyes and yawned. All three mice snored softly, tired out from travel and the excitement of finding each other again.

By the time Nicholas woke up, it was late in the day. The sun was once again setting across the lake behind the Adirondack Mountains of New York State. As Nicholas lay there trying to wake up, he remembered his friend Edward had gone off to New York. He wondered if the gulls found Edward. He wondered if they gave Edward the message to come to Burlington.

He looked at his brother still sleeping quietly curled up on a bed of lilac leaves. Then he looked where his uncle had fallen asleep. Nicholas jumped up. "Oh, no," he shouted. "Uncle William, where are you?" He shook his brother. "Clarence, wake up," Nicholas said. "Where did Uncle William go?"

Nicholas ran out into the park. A woman walked her dog along the curving path overlooking the lake. A family, sitting on a blanket under a tree, set out a picnic dinner. Two boys played catch with a ball and gloves. Nicholas didn't see his uncle anywhere. He turned back to his brother.

Nicholas heard the two boys shouting and wondered what was going on. He headed back into the park. The boys had dropped the ball and gloves and were running around stooped over. They had their hands out and flopped down on the ground, cupping something as they fell. One boy stood up and shouted, "I got him, I got him!" The other boy tugged on the first boy's shirt. "Let me see, let me see," he said.

Nicholas couldn't see what the boys had caught. He was afraid he knew. He crept as close as he dare to where

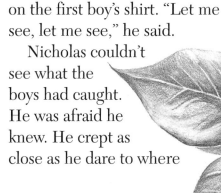

the family was picnicking. "Now boys, don't bring that awful thing near our food," the mother said. "I have heard they carry diseases."

Nicholas looked from behind a bush and saw the boy with something cupped in his hands. It was Uncle William. His tail stuck out from one side of the boy's hands and his head stuck out from the other side. He had a most unhappy expression on his face. Nicholas wanted to laugh. He was happy he found his uncle, but he had to help him escape.

Nicholas thought about going to get his brother. Together they would figure out a plan. Nicholas didn't want to leave his uncle in case the family decided to leave the park. He looked first at the lilac bush where his brother slept, then back toward the boys holding his uncle. They were both looking up at the spreading maple tree.

"I think it is trying to get our attention," one boy said.

"Chipmunks aren't smart enough for that," the other boy said. He still held Uncle William in his hands. The chipmunk stamped his paw on the branch and leapt down to the ground. The boys chased after him. Nicholas watched them take off through the park. He followed along behind. The chipmunk looked familiar.

When the chipmunk saw the boys had gotten away from the picnic, he stopped. He turned around and started chasing after the boys. They were not used to small animals behaving in such a way. They dropped the mouse on the ground and ran as fast as they could back toward their family. The mouse and chipmunk ran off into the trees.

"I have to thank you," Uncle William said to the chipmunk. "You can never tell what boys will do."

"Nonsense," the chipmunk said. "It was really no trouble. I have been rescuing a small mouse friend of my own for some time now. I kind of got separated from him recently. I had a bit of an adventure of my own you might say."

"Are you Edward?" Uncle William asked. "My nephew Nicholas has told me all about you. I have news about his parents. They have been caught and are living in a glass cage with a family in Woodstock. I need Nicholas's help to rescue them."

"I am indeed Edward," he said. "Where is that little mouse? Does he know about his parents yet?"

"I am right here," Nicholas said. He came running up to his uncle and Edward. He had a big smile on his face when he realized both Uncle William and Edward were right here and safe. "What do you mean, do I know about my parents yet? Uncle William, you have to tell me the whole story. Clarence will want to hear this, too."

William, Edward, and Nicholas walked in a wide circle away from the picnicking family and headed back to where Clarence waited under the lilac bush.

Chapter Twenty-Three

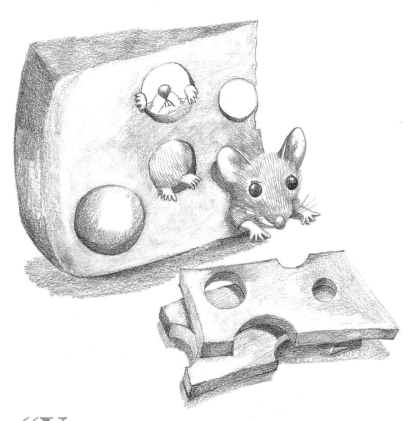

"Your parents were worried about you, Nicholas," William said. "They waited and waited for you to return to the farm in Stockbridge." The mice were sitting in the shade of a big lilac bush overlooking Lake Champlain.

"When I left your house in West Tisbury," Nicholas said, "you were going to head out to my parents to tell them I was all right but heading off to Maine. What happened?"

"I had a long trip out to the western part of Massachusetts. I'm not as young as I used to be, so it took me a long time to reach the farm."

"What did my parents say when you got there?" Nicholas asked.

"They were relieved to hear you were all right. I told them where you were and not to worry. I sent your friend Edward off to help you."

"That's right," Edward said. "I was enjoying a quiet visit with my own family when William came through town. Of course I headed right out to help you in Maine, Nicholas."

"When I got to Stockbridge," William said, "I spent the whole summer with your parents. Finally, when you didn't come home by fall, we decided to look for you. Clarence, they knew you lived in Vermont so they headed up this way to ask you to help look for Nicholas. That's when it happened."

"What happened to our parents?" Clarence asked. "They never made it as far as north as my old barn." William looked at the two brothers.

"Your parents were trapped and taken away," William said. "I just missed getting caught myself." William looked down at the ground. He had a sheepish look on his face. "Well, we couldn't help ourselves really. We were headed for a tasty smelling cheese shop, this state is full of them you know, when your parents fell for the oldest trick in the book."

"Did they get caught in a trap?" Clarence asked.

"We were all so hungry, and the cheese looked so yummy. Your parents ran right into the end of the open trap. Last I saw them, they were holding the piece of cheese in their paws when the trap door swung shut. If I wasn't so slow, I would have been right in there with them."

"But they were still all right when you last saw them?" Nicholas asked.

"Yes, they looked a bit frightened but they were together and safe inside the trap," William said.

"We don't have a moment to lose," Nicholas said. "We need to rescue them. There is no telling what will become of them if they stay cooped up in the trap."

"Nicholas, what about looking for Francis?" Clarence said. "You have been looking for him for a long time. Maybe I should keep looking for him, while you go rescue Mom and Dad?"

Nicholas looked at his brother. He had almost forgotten about the family journal and Francis. He thought for a while, then made a decision. "What good are a bunch of old stories if we forget about our family now?" Nicholas said. "After we rescue Mom and Dad, then we can look for Francis."

"If you are sure, then we need to get going," William said. "It is a long way to Woodstock from here, and we don't have any way to get there except walking."

"I'm ready to start if you are," Clarence said.

The three mice and Edward left the shade of the lilac bush and walked out into the sunshine of Battery Park. Looking east toward the city, all three animals stopped. They could see the blocks of the city give way to the campus of the state university and more mountains in the distance.

"We better find another way to travel," Nicholas said. "There is just too much ground to cover."

As they moved east out of the city, Edward noticed an old red airplane with one wing over another parked on a runway of a small airport. A pilot wiped his brow and set his cap down. He discussed flying to the state capital as he gassed up the plane.

"I say," Clarence said, "now that plane looks like just the thing to get us quickly to Montpelier." The others agreed, but Uncle William didn't see how it would be possible for all of them to get on the plane without the pilot noticing.

"Don't worry about a thing," Edward said. "I will take care of the pilot. The rest of you get ready to run for the plane."

The animals were hiding in a patch of thistles beside the runway. Edward leapt right out onto the tar and ran right up to the pilot. He grabbed the pilot's cap in his teeth and ran off. The pilot ran off after the chipmunk and his cap.

"This is our chance," Nicholas said. "Come on." The mice scrambled out onto the tar and up the wheels of the old plane. They hid in the front seat of the open plane. Soon the pilot came back with his hat on and climbed aboard the plane. He started the engine and the big propeller began to turn.

"What about Edward?" Uncle William said to the others when they heard the plane starting.

"Don't worry about him," Nicholas said. "He won't be left behind."

The chubby chipmunk scampered out onto the runway as the plane taxied by. Edward made a leap for the passing wheel and just managed to hold on to the struts above the wheel as the plane took off.

"Nicholas," Edward shouted, as he looked down at the fast moving ground beneath him, "this better be a short flight."

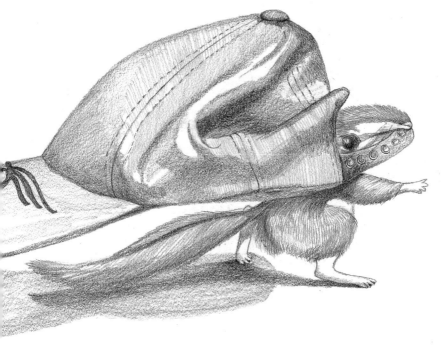

Chapter Twenty-Four

The red biplane landed with a bump after what was, indeed, a short flight. On one side, they had passed Mount Mansfield, the highest mountain in the state. The Camel's Hump passed on the other, unseen by the animals in the plane. Nicholas, Clarence, and Uncle William spent their time curled up in the front cockpit under an old blanket.

Edward saw every tree and hill on the flight. He stood on a crossbar under the plane and gripped a control wire with all his might. His brown fur flapped in the wind and his tail streamed out straight behind. The short flight convinced Edward that flying was truly for the birds.

When the pilot had gone into the airport, the mice escaped from the plane and found Edward laying in the tall grass, wild chicory, and red clover. He was staring up at a sky filling in with dark clouds. He rested there until he noticed his friends standing around him.

"There you are, Edward," Nicholas said. "I thought

you were off on another adventure on your own again. I'm glad you made the plane with us."

"Nicholas, you are my friend, but the next time we have to travel a long distance, can we do it on the ground?"

"Come on, Edward," Nicholas said, "we have to find out where we are." The animals helped Edward get up and they headed off in search of directions to Woodstock. They made their way toward a city down in a valley. When the sun peaked through the gathering clouds, it flashed off the golden dome of a tall building.

"I think I know where we are," Clarence said. "I passed through when I first moved up here." Big raindrops started to fall as they walked through the city. They stopped and looked up at a long green lawn. A bright garden of Canna lilies and snapdragons grew near the street. A massive granite building stood at the far end of the grass.

"This is Montpelier, the state capital," Clarence said. "I bet we can find out how to get to Woodstock from here."

Rain was falling steadily now. The animals were hungry and wanted to find a place to dry off. They headed for the large, pillared building at the end of the lawn. All four animals stopped at once, standing in the rain at the bottom of the long flight of granite steps.

"I don't like the looks of that statue up there," Nicholas said. They huddled under the edge of the first step and debated what to do.

"It is just a statue," William said. "It can't bother us. I want to get out of this rain."

"I don't know," Clarence said. "There is something kind of scary about him."

"Well, we have to do something," Edward said. "I need to dry out my fur. It still hasn't been the same since that plane ride."

"Look, let's go over there," Nicholas said. He pointed to a tall building next to the state capitol building. "There are big porches, and plenty of places for us to dry off."

Everyone ran between the raindrops across the lawn and up the long flight of steps. Nicholas took one last look at the statue of Ethan Allen standing on the front steps of the capitol. He shivered in the cold rain.

No one seemed to be around on the big porch of the building next to the capitol. They sniffed out a way inside the dark building. Nicholas squeaked and jumped when his eyes adjusted to the dim light.

"What is that?" he asked, pointing to a big cat looking at them. It didn't move.

Uncle William stepped forward and sniffed at the cat. "I'd say he's stuffed," William said.

"This kind of panther used to roam the state years ago," Clarence said. "I've heard them called catamounts. Lucky for us, they aren't around anymore."

"Well, at least this one looks safe," Edward said. "I

wouldn't want to meet one of those in the wild." They moved on as a group into the dark building.

"This seems to be all about the state of Vermont," William said. They wandered through a native shelter set up inside the building. The collection of furs hanging inside the building made the small animals uneasy. They quickly moved through images of old farms, vast herds of sheep, and railroads chugging along through the mountains.

Edward slowed his walk while he looked at the pictures of cheese and butter making.

"Is anyone else getting hungry? It seems as though I haven't eaten in weeks."

"Come on, Edward," Nicholas said. "We can eat when we find out how to get to Woodstock." It was Nicholas's turn to slow down when he saw pictures of a great flood that happened in Vermont years ago. It reminded him of the flood he went through back home— the whole reason he was on this journey now.

"Come on, everyone, we need to find a map or something," he said.

"Don't worry, Nicholas," Clarence said. "Our parents will be fine. This is just what we are looking for." They stopped in front of a large map of Vermont hanging on the wall.

"There it is!" Nicholas shouted. He pointed with his paw to a spot on the map. It was south and east of where they were right now.

"That doesn't seem so far away," Nicholas said.

Chapter Twenty-Five

The four animals made their way south from Montpelier. They rested when they were tired. They ate when they could find food. The seasons were changing in Vermont. Summer passed and the air turned cooler. Trees turned shades of red, orange, and yellow.

Clarence tried to find a path south. They followed many small valleys and climbed over tall hills. All the time, unknown to them, their southward progress was leading them deeper into the Green Mountains.

Soon they were in a dark forest of maples, oaks, and beech trees. Uncle William yawned and sat down near a clump of black-eyed Susans growing in the forest. "I think we have walked enough today," he said. The other animals stopped and sat near him. They all agreed.

A cold wind blew up the mountainside. Edward shivered. "It is getting late, Nicholas. I suspect we will have snow soon. Are you sure we are going in the right direction?"

Clarence said, "They call these the Green Mountains but they will be covered in snow soon."

"I am not sure we are going the right way at all," Nicholas said. "I think we are heading south."

"Well, you wouldn't know it by the weather. It feels like winter more than ever here," Edward said. Almost as soon as Edward spoke, big white flakes drifted down through the trees. They made a soft patting sound on the dry leaves scattered on the ground. "You know," Edward said, "it might be wise to keep moving. They will find us in the spring, topped with snow like so many cakes sitting in a row."

"You are right," Uncle William said. "It is getting dark. I don't like to be out in the woods at night without shelter. Who knows what is lurking among the trees."

The animals got moving again, but they were now looking for a place to spend the night. They found a great spruce tree that had been struck by lightning years ago. The dead trunk was mostly hollow, with an empty knothole on one side.

The animals settled inside the tree. They talked for a while about where they might be and how to find their way to Woodstock. It didn't take long for the tired animals to drop off one-by-one. Nicholas was the last awake. He peered out the knothole into the darkness.

On the ground he glimpsed a small animal struggling along with something.

The forest was full of night sounds. The animals that sleep during the day and search for food at night were all up and about their business. The snow had stopped earlier. It slid off the trees here and there with a clumpf sound. The ground had a clean but thin carpet of white that made it easier for Nicholas to see.

Nicholas crawled out of the tree and down to the ground. He found the tracks of the animal he saw from the tree right away. Sure enough, the tracks belonged to a mouse. Nicholas followed the tracks for a while. He was getting farther from the tree with his friends. Up ahead in the gloom, he noticed the mouse moving slowly. He dragged something along making a trail in the snow next to his paw prints.

Nicholas stopped to try and focus on the animal. "Francis?" Nicholas said quietly. "Is that you, Francis?"

The mouse ahead of him moved on a few paces, then stopped. He didn't turn to look at Nicholas for a moment. Nicholas took a few steps toward the mouse. A great clump of snow fell off a tree branch between Nicholas and the other mouse.

When the snow had settled, the other mouse had started traveling again. Nicholas followed. He was about to catch the mouse and he reached out to touch what Nicholas believed was their family journal when he heard a blood-curdling scream coming from deep in the forest. Both mice froze.

The first mouse ran off. They heard another scream, this one closer. Nicholas ran as fast as he could to catch up with the mouse. Ahead, the mouse had stopped at the base of a tree, peeking over a root back at Nicholas.

"Don't follow me, Nicholas. The cat can smell us both. You have to go the other way, hurry."

Nicholas paused for a moment. "Francis, it is you. Where are you going with our journal?"

"It is my journal now," Francis said. "I am going to Woodstock. I know your parents are there. They will let me keep the journal. Now run, the cat is near." Francis didn't wait to hear Nicholas's reply. He took off into the deep dark woods. Nicholas was about to follow him when the biggest cat he had ever seen slowly walked into his view.

Nicholas froze for a moment. His whiskers quivered. His fur stood up on end. This was a real live catamount. The stuffed one in the museum was scary to look at, but this was entirely different. The cat looked right at the little mouse with his yellow eyes. Its thick tail twitched back and forth slowly. It seemed to be purring quietly to itself.

With one quick movement, the cat leapt. Nicholas left the spot the cat would land in and ran as fast as he had ever run before. Nicholas kicked up snow and leaves as he ran. The cat followed, swinging his head from side-to-side to see clearly. Nicholas made his way back to the dead tree. All he could think to do was climb back up and hide.

The cat was gaining fast on the mouse. Nicholas was at the dead tree. He looked up. The other animals were awake and bouncing on a dead branch near the opening of their knothole. Nicholas leapt for the tree. The cat reached out with his great front paw. The animals in the tree bounced on the branch.

There was a crack, and the animals screamed and leapt for the knothole. Nicholas ran up the side of the tree. There was a yowl as the branch fell on the great catamount's head. Nicholas dove back inside the knothole. His friends cheered and hugged Nicholas. The catamount slinked away to find an easier meal.

Chapter Twenty-Six

The four friends waited until the sun was well up in the sky before they left the safety of their knothole. Nicholas peeked out all morning, afraid the big cat would come back. When the sun had melted the snow off the trees, the animals crept down to the forest floor.

Clarence and Nicholas led the other two out from the trees. They were high on a rolling hill. An old stone wall followed the tree line. Some young trees grew on the downhill side of the wall. In the valley, a few farms stood out from the fields and forests. Another mountain rose up on the far side of the valley.

"I would dearly love a ride," Edward said. "Something safe and close to the ground."

"Cheer up, all," Uncle William said. "We are making progress in the right direction. I am sure we must be getting close." He squinted up at the mountains all around him "Well, at least I think we are making progress."

They traveled on through the Green Mountains, sometimes climbing right up and over mountains. Sometimes they made their way around the sides of the steeply sloped ground. The weather grew colder.

It snowed every few days. It collected in deep drifts. The small animals were unable to make much progress. They traveled the length of the mountains. One cold, snowy day Nicholas stopped and couldn't move any more. The others looked back and saw the little mouse shivering in the gray light. A sound echoed through the trees.

Clarence recognized the noise first. It was the distant sound of dogs barking. All four animals scurried over to the edge of the trail. Soon the baying voices came much closer. A pack of dogs, pulling a sled, skidded around a bend in the trail.

The lead dog, smiling and running with his pink tongue hanging out, barked and came to a stop. The other dogs stopped in a tangle of lines. The woman riding on the sled walked up to see what was going on. Daniel was sniffing about in the snow bank. He barked short sharp tones.

"Nicholas," Daniel said, "is that you?" What are you doing in the Green Mountains in the winter?"

"Oh, Daniel," Nicholas said, "am I glad to see you. We are kind of lost out here. This is my brother, uncle, and Edward. Can you give us a ride?"

"My, my," Daniel said. "Your group just grows and grows. Quick, jump under the blanket on the sled. The driver won't notice while she is busy with the other dogs."

The animals wasted no time snuggling down under the warm wool blanket strapped to the sled. When the musher came back and called out, the dogs tugged on their lines and pulled the sled forward with a jerk. Nicholas fell asleep right away, curled up next to the others.

Nicholas woke up to his uncle nudging him with a paw. The sled had stopped. It was dark and they were on level ground again. "Come now, Nicholas. It is time for us to move on. Daniel says Woodstock is really over the next hill now. Mount Tom is over there and that one is called Mount Peg."

"We have made it?" Nicholas asked. "Are we really in Woodstock?" He jumped up from the warm blanket.

Daniel was eating his dinner by firelight. "Oh, thank you, Daniel," Nicholas said. "You have saved us. We would have wandered around in those woods until we froze."

"Glad to do it," Daniel said, between mouthfuls of food. "Now you best be getting down to town. Look for the Green. It's a big oval park. It's right in the middle of town."

All four animals thanked Daniel and followed Nicholas. They found the twinkling lights of the brick and clapboard village houses lining the streets. Stone-faced stores, closed this late at night, offered dim light to the searching animals. They looked in the window of a large old hardware store. Their reflections looked back at them.

"Uncle William," Nicholas said, "how are we going to find my parents in this town? They could be in any one of these houses, or even in this big store."

"Now don't worry about a thing, young Nicholas. Let's find a place to rest and get something to eat. I am sure after a little sleep the very answer we need will come to us."

Nicholas looked back at his reflection in the window. He was not the little mouse who left home so long ago. He could see he had gotten bigger and older. If his parents were to be saved, he knew he would be the one who would have to do it. He saw the others turn and follow William to search out a place to sleep. He looked away from his reflection and went the other way to find his parents.

Chapter Twenty-Seven

Nicholas went from home to home in Woodstock. The old houses in town were decorated for Christmas. Evergreen wreaths hung from the doors and white candles glowed in the windows. He peeked into windows. He listened at doors. He hoped to see or hear something that would tell him where his parents were.

Uncle William and the others were searching for other animals that might know something helpful. Nicholas trudged along by himself. He stayed near the town green. He tried to stay out of the way of shoppers as they ducked into and out of stores looking for last-minute gifts. A little girl and her mother came out of Gillingham's.

The mother balanced an armful of packages as she towed her daughter along behind with her other hand. Nicholas watched from near the steps of the store. "Come along Gillian, we have a lot to do today."

"But, Mom," Gillian was saying, "I want to get a present for the mice. They look sad. Can we buy them a present?" Nicholas perked up at her words. The mother stopped and thought over her answer. "You haven't paid much attention to your new pets for some time," Gillian's mom said. "Maybe we should get the mice some nice flax seed for Christmas." Gillian held the door for her mother and they went back into the old hardware store.

Nicholas wanted to know more about the mice and where the mother and daughter lived. He waited outside for them to return. Soon Gillian and her mom pushed the door open. Gillian swung a paper bag with a green-and-red bow in her hand. "I am going to find a little stocking for them. One for the boy and one for the girl," Gillian said. The mother and daughter walked along the sidewalk to their home.

Nicholas dodged the feet of other shoppers as he followed Gillian and her mom home. They walked through the green to a white clapboard-covered house. Gillian had made a snowman in her front yard. He held an old ski pole in one snow arm and he wore a black-and-red checked hat.

"Hello, Mr. Snowflake," Gillian called as they arrived home. The big brass knocker in the middle of an evergreen wreath clanked as they shut the front door.

Nicholas hid behind Mr. Snowflake. He had to see inside the house. He was sure his parents were in there.

He looked all around the house. It was neat and clean and well cared for. He didn't find a single opening big enough for a mouse. He went around again. He heard the door open at the side of the house. The father had a bundle of trash and was headed for the garage. When he returned, his arms loaded with firewood, Nicholas scooted inside just as the kitchen door slammed behind him.

Nicholas knew enough to head for cover as soon as he was inside the house. Sometimes people were kind of jumpy when they see a mouse in their house. Nicholas listened for voices from the family. They all seemed to be in the big living room. Nicholas could smell a wood fire and the scent of the forest.

They were decorating the Christmas tree. Nicholas scampered across the hardwood floor. He didn't dare call out for his parents. He didn't want the family to hear his squeaking. He looked in room after room on the first floor. No cage, no mice, no luck.

Nicholas headed up the stairs. He heard a shriek from the living room. He looked back and saw the mother pointing at the stairs. "Gillian, your mice are out of their cage again," the mother said.

Nicholas jumped up the stairs without looking back. He ran down a long hallway to an ajar door and ducked inside. He ran around a pile of discarded clothes, jumped over a doll having tea, and hid behind a big desk in the corner of the room.

The father opened the door to the girl's room. He looked at the cage on the desk. "Well, I'll be," he said to himself, "the mice are inside. He must have found a way to get in and out of the cage," the father shouted down to the rest of his family. "This will stop you," he said to the mice, as he placed a stack of books on top of the screen blocking the top of the glass cage and left the room.

When he couldn't hear footsteps, Nicholas crept out from under the desk. He looked up at the glass cage. He could not see inside from where he stood. He made his way up a sweater draped over the back of the desk chair. He stood on the back of the chair and looked into the cage. There they were.

The bottom of the cage was filled with cedar shavings. Nicholas's mother, Marilyn, sat looking out at her son. His father, Henry, sat in the bottom of an exercise wheel. It rolled back and forth like Henry had just been running on it. They both had a look of surprise, then recognition, on their faces.

"Mom, Dad," Nicholas called from the chair. "I'm here! I found you at last! Don't worry, I'll get you out."

Chapter Twenty-Eight

Nicholas was alone in the room with his parents. They stood in the glass cage. A water bottle dripped into a small dish. A few flax seeds lay in the bottom of a food bowl. His mother twitched her nose and her whiskers buzzed trying to sense Nicholas. His father stood beside her, so glad to see his long-missing son.

"I'll get you out, don't worry," Nicholas said. "I will be back in a minute."

Nicholas jumped down from the chair. He hit the floor and was out the door. His parents held each other and looked up at the screen holding them in the cage. They scratched at the glass walls again. Their little paws didn't leave a mark.

Nicholas paced the hallway outside. He was trying to think. He wished Edward were with him. Even Uncle William or Clarence would have an idea, Nicholas thought. He tried to think about all the adventures he'd had. He knew something would help him. He thought back to the very reason he was on this journey. First there was the flood at home, then his family's escape, and his long trip in search of the journal.

Nicholas looked back into the room and the cage. Slowly another drip of water fell out of the water bottle. A thought came to him. "Maybe it will work," he said out loud. Nicholas had a plan.

William, Edward, and Clarence were wandering up and down the streets of Woodstock. They called out for Nicholas and they peeked in windows looking for his parents. Behind them another mouse followed quietly. He didn't say anything. He wanted to find Nicholas's parents, too.

Inside the house, Nicholas was looking for something to make his plan work. He was just a small mouse, but getting his parents out of the cage gave him great courage and strength. He ran back inside Gillian's room and looked up at the desk. From the chair, Gillian could look out the window at the snow silently falling outside.

Nicholas jumped for the chair. From there, he leapt over to a bookcase and climbed up the big picture books to the top. He tugged and tugged at a long book about horses. It flopped out of the case and landed on the cage, leaning against the window.

"Ha, ha," Nicholas shouted, "I got the first step in place."

His parents looked up at Nicholas through the wire screen. "Nicholas, what are you doing?" his father asked. "Don't put more books on top of the screen."

"Don't worry, Dad," Nicholas said. "I have a plan. It might take a little while, but I think I can get you out of that cage."

Nicholas scrambled up the book leaning against the window. He reached the window latch and pushed. It was stuck. He pushed again with his back against the window and his paws pushing on the latch. He slowly swung around. The top window was unlatched. Without the latch to hold it up, the top window slid down, leaving the book poking out the open window.

"Now, watch out, I am going out onto the roof. Please don't worry, I'll be careful," Nicholas said.

He wasted no time in scrambling up the side of the house. He used all four paws to hold onto the building. He made it up to the roof. The snow had been piling up out here in the cold. His breath came out in puffs of steam. Nicholas began to shove snow off the roof. It fell down the side of the house in clumps.

Some of the snow caught on the book sticking out

of the window. It landed inside the warm room and melted right away. The slushy water slid down the book and splashed inside the cage. Nicholas's parents had to jump to the far corner. They hid behind the food dish. The bottom of the cage was filling with water.

Nicholas, still on the roof shoving snow over the edge, heard voices down on the ground. "Nicholas, what are you doing up on that roof?" It was Uncle William and the others. They spied the little mouse hard at work.

"I found them," Nicholas shouted. "I need all your help. We need more snow."

The other animals climbed up the side of the house and met Nicholas on the roof. Patches of stars showed through the snow clouds. A stray flake fell now and again.

Edward was the first to speak. "Is it your parents, Nicholas?" he asked. "Are they in this house?"

"Yes. I don't have time to explain, just help me shove the snow off this roof."

The animals, holding tightly to the roof with their paws, pushed and shoved snow down the slope and over the edge. Some fell to the ground but some caught on the book and melted in the room. The water continued to collect inside the cage. Henry and Marilyn were now inside the food dish. It floated in the shallow water.

On the roof, the animals laughed and joked about

who could get the most snow off the roof at once. Clarence nearly slid off when he pushed a big pile of snow that had collected near the chimney. The clouds were breaking up and the night sky was filled with stars.

Inside the house, the family finished decorating their tree. Gillian felt cold and shivered. Her mother noticed. "I feel a draft," she said. "It feels like someone left a window open." She went to see where the breeze was coming from.

The little mouse that had followed the other animals to this house found his own way in and was creeping along the baseboard in the hall.

In Gillian's room, the cage was filling fast with water and snow. The mice were safe in their dish, but their heads bumped against the screen at the top now and again. "Just a bit more snow should do it," Henry shouted out to his son up on the roof.

Gillian's mom walked up the stairs, feeling the draft getting stronger as she climbed.

The cage was now full. The food dish bumped against the screen. With each added clump of snow it jiggled the books on top. A tiny seam on the edge of the cage started to leak. A small stream of water ran out onto the floor. Henry looked down at it. Would the cage empty before enough water filled it to move the screen?

Gillian's mom stopped at the door to Gillian's room. "I think I found the draft," she shouted down to her daughter. "What on earth have you been doing?" she asked over her shoulder.

As she spoke, the little mouse leapt into the room. It was Francis. He had the journal. He held it up to Henry and Marilyn. "I have the journal," he shouted. "Tell Nicholas it is mine."

The water, full to the top of the cage, shifted the screen enough for Marilyn and Henry to leap out and over to the bookcase. As they leapt, the cage burst with a CRACK. The water poured out and onto the floor.

Francis looked up at the noise. He held the journal over his head and the water rushed down, soaking him and the journal.

Gillian's mom shrieked, slammed the door, and ran back down the hall. Nicholas and the others on the roof made their way into the room. Nicholas ran to his parents.

They all rejoiced and gathered in Clarence and Uncle William. Edward poked around the broken food dish. Francis held up limp pages of the journal.

Epilogue

The mouse family had a joyful reunion. They ran from the house and hid in the back of the big hardware store. Marilyn hugged and hugged her son. She and Henry told Nicholas all about fixing up their house in the Berkshires after the flood. Uncle William described his journey to the farm after Nicholas left for Maine. They all talked about waiting and waiting to hear from Nicholas.

Clarence, who had been away from his home for so long, smiled and listened to the stories of the old owl in the forest above the farm. He remembered when Kip, the sheep dog, was a pup and Shirley was a young lamb skipping over the meadow. He talked about his own home on the farm in northern Vermont.

Francis worried over the pieces of the journal. He

tried to carefully dry each one. He kept what was left of the journal tucked away in a secret hiding place that only he knew about. When no one was looking, he strained to read what was left of the old stories. He nearly forgot the other members of his family who were so happy all around him.

Edward sat back and enjoyed the mouse family reunion. He kept his paws on his belly, chuckling when Nicholas told a tale from their travels. He shivered when Nicholas talked about the dangers they had faced together. He thought he might like to travel on his own next time. He had heard some amazing stories about a huge city somewhere in New York.

"Nicholas," his father said, "we are so proud and amazed at everything you survived for our old family stories. I am glad you are safe with us again."

"I am, too," his mother said. "You were smart and brave and found a good friend." Nicholas lost count of the number of times she had hugged him.

"But the journal," Nicholas said, "I was supposed to bring a copy home for us to save our old family stories. The journal is mostly ruined."

Nicholas's parents looked over at Francis, who was trying to read a word off a small bit of paper. "Never mind that old journal. We will always remember the stories that are important to us," Henry said.

"Besides," Marilyn added, "when we get home, you can begin a new journal. It will start with the amazing adventures of Nicholas the mouse."

mitten press

Mitten Press is pleased to present the conclusion of this series of chapter books about a lively field mouse from Massachusetts. He lives tucked under a farmhouse outside Stockbridge until a flood destroys the journal that contains his family history. In Book One, Nicholas embarks on a journey across Massachusetts to locate his long-lost uncle and a copy of the precious journal. Book Two sees Nicholas depart for Maine after finding out that his cousin has taken the journal copy there. As Nicholas will discover, Maine is a very large and diverse state. In Book Three, Nicholas and his friend Edward the chipmunk travel to the mountains of New Hampshire, following a trail of clues left by Nicholas's cousin Francis. In his final adventure in Book Four, Nicholas and Edward become separated from Francis and follow his trail through the state of Vermont.

The series chronicles Nicholas's adventures throughout New England. In each book, young readers learn about another state—the animals that live there, the geography, and even the state's history—as Nicholas continues searching for his family journal.

This is Daniel.

I met Jillian

The Adv

B